DIESEL

First Edition

Published by The Nazca Plains Corporation
Las Vegas, Nevada
2009

ISBN: 978-1-935509-29-5

Published by

The Nazca Plains Corporation ®
4640 Paradise Rd, Suite 141
Las Vegas NV 89109-8000

PUBLISHER'S NOTE
DIESEL is a work of fiction created wholly by *Allen Giffen's* imagination. All characters are fictional and any resemblance to any persons living or deceased is purely by accident. No portion of this book reflects any real person or events.

Cover Photos
Andrey Vishnyakov and Simon Bachofen

Art Director
Blake Stephens

DEDICATION

This book is dedicated to all the Diesels of the world. May you always be there to fuel our fantasies and every once in a while, turn them into reality.

DIESEL

First Edition

Allen Giffen

CHAPTER 1

Making the Grade

"What the fuck is it with Diesel?" a frustrated Tom Koehler thought as he sat at his kitchen table in his robe on a Sunday evening. To augment his high school teaching salary, Tom taught at Texas A& M each summer. Divorced and paying child support put him in a position where he didn't have much of a choice. The daily drive wasn't too bad and the term was almost over.

Tom had been teaching high school English in Texas for the last 14 years, and summers at Texas A&M for the last 5. He considered himself pretty normal and average. But Diesel was putting a twist into that perspective. The short version was that Tom was having a difficult time accepting his growing physical attraction for Diesel. Tom had been a jock in high school and college, excelling in track especially. Never at a loss for pussy when he wanted it, females flocked around him all the time. Guys hit on him regularly too, but he just laughed it off. His ex-wife had been a cheerleader at his college. The sex with her had always been great, but it wasn't enough to allow their marriage to survive adding a child to the mix and dealing with frequent financial ups and downs.

1

Tom kept in shape now mainly by running regularly, but he also used his high school gym equipment and pool, and there were even better facilities he could use in the summer at the college — at 43, he looked pretty good. He believed the only good thing since his divorce 2 years earlier was that he was free to have sex again with lots of women — and he did. But it was starting to bore him.

As his teaching career progressed, one of the things he became aware of was that he started appreciating the hot tight bodies of some of his students. First, just the girls. All a girl had to do was bend over anywhere within his eyeshot and if they were wearing low cut jeans or shorts and he caught sight of any kind of thong underwear strap, he got wood — didn't matter what he was doing. He also had a thing for big tits. And the way some of these young girls could have great big jugs that seemed to hold up so firmly on their own, well, he always considered women's tits to be two of the Seven Wonders of the World, and he'd harden up.

With the guys, it was different, or so Tom thought. He would often see his students and other teen guys naked in the school locker room or shower after an after school workout session in the shared faculty/student gym, and was not embarrassed about checking them out. A favorite activity was picturing himself with the perfect body by mentally morphing body parts from different kids onto himself — Billy Summers' ass (Tom ranked it high because it was a bubble butt and because when he walked, his butt muscles flexed in such a way that the sides of his cheeks rippled in and out, as if they were breathing or something), Derek Anderson's dick (cut, perfectly shaped with a large head, at least 4 inches soft with huge hanging balls — though there had been others in the running, what gave Derek's cock the blue ribbon was the one time Tom saw it hard in the showers — long and thick with a head that looked like a big mushroom on top of a bratwurst), little Gary Miller's chest (on his 5'5" frame, Gary's very well developed chest looked almost freakish, especially when exposed – Tom took note of the stares Gary sometimes got in the hallways on days when he'd wear a tight t-shirt — it was difficult to accept visually that a chest that huge could narrow itself down to a waist as tiny as Gary's), Max Weldon's legs (Max was a weightlifter who always wore sweatpants or really baggy pants at school, as if he wanted to hide what his legs looked like. In the gym though, under the gaze of plenty of admiring eyes, he would proudly expose his tree trunk legs — they could almost hypnotize you if you watched them as he walked, how the muscles rolled over each other under Max' skin), and so on. But his fantasizing about students seemed to kick into a higher gear since the divorce and newly rediscovered freedom.

Part of the problem, which was very slowly creeping into Tom's consciousness, was that in Diesel, he was seeing a collection of body parts that pretty much topped the chart in all areas. Diesel had already completed 4 years of college, but would be around for at least another one, maybe two, because he was in no hurry to graduate. At first Tom attributed Diesel's casual demeanor in class to some kind of territorial marking the guy did to impress the rest of the class — typical male hormonal shit. At first he wasn't real sure that Diesel was playing him. He was soon to learn what a master player Diesel is. Though he'd run into Diesel a few times in the locker room, it was always when one of them was leaving and the other arriving. Tom often wondered what Diesel looked like in the buff.

As he sat at the kitchen table drinking his third beer, his mind again went over the scene he witnessed earlier that afternoon. He was able to get some grading and computer work done in peace on weekends at the school, in an office the university supplied for faculty who only taught there in the summer. About 2pm that day, he figured he'd done enough and packed up. About to step onto the stairs to go down, he stopped in his tracks when he glanced at the security mirror hanging a half flight down.

He'd worn gym shoes and had been engrossed in thought as he approached the open stairwell and the two guys in the mirror didn't see him. Tom slowly moved backwards, into the shadows of the hall, but was still able to clearly see the mirror.

They were a half flight further down, Diesel with his back to the wall facing the mirror, t-shirt pulled over his head, pressing at the back of his neck, arms resting at his side, eyes shut, mouth slack. He had an old pair of chinos on. Leaning into him was a kid Tom didn't recognize — noticeably smaller than Diesel. The kid had a hand on each of Diesel's pecs, squeezing them; his mouth was open and rubbing around the hills and valleys of Diesel's abs. The kid was moaning pretty loudly. One hand let go of a nipple, slowly slid down Diesel's torso, and disappeared.

"Not the hog, asshole!" said Diesel to the kid's face. Diesel had grabbed the kid by the hair and pulled him off his body. "You paid for this," said Diesel as he used his other hand indicating his torso, "not the hog," as he rubbed his crotch. "If you want to touch the hog, you're gonna have to pay five times what you're payin' now. Its fine to lay on it while playin' with my chest, just don't grab it with your hands. Do it again, and your 10 minutes ends now."

Tom realized he'd been holding his breath. He was amazed at how forceful Diesel was being. And the way Diesel seemed to be so casual about using his body. And what a body! Though Tom had a pretty good idea what Diesel was carrying around on and with him, this was the first time he was seeing Diesel's torso in the flesh. Even from that distance, and reflected in a mirror, it looked to Tom like Diesel's chest and abs were both huge and hard. But not as hard as Tom's dick right then.

"Times up, Sean," said Diesel as he pushed the kid away.

"Please, Diesel, please, just another minute, I was almost there," Sean pleaded while panting. "I'll pay double next time...please?"

Diesel jammed his hands inside the waist of his chinos, forcing the waist down slightly. "Sean, you'll pay whatever I say it's gonna cost, and you'll do it when I let you do it. Got it? It's your own damned fault that you can't cum fast enough. Move!" Diesel pushed the kid to the side and walked away pulling his t-shirt back on. Sean followed soon after.

Tom sat at his kitchen table, paying no attention to the fact that while going over the story in his mind, he'd once again gotten hard, grabbed his cock, and was stroking it. The image of Diesel leaning

4

back on the wall, eyes closed, with that Sean kid worshipping him was burned into his mind. He was pounding his cock. The cum flew out in great spurts underneath the table, each accompanied by a grunt. Tom even heard a couple of spurts land with a splat on the tile floor.

A minute later, he was under the table wiping the puddles of cum up with some paper towels, he felt a cold drop on his neck, stopped, and looked up. "Holy fuck!" he said out loud as he noticed a glob of cum above him. Apparently, at least a couple of his shots were strong enough to first shoot upwards onto the bottom of the table.

"I gotta get that kid out of my mind."

It was the last week of the summer session. Everyone seemed happy it was coming to a close. It was a somewhat remedial English class; most of the students were freshmen or sophomores. Diesel was the oldest in the class. The first three weeks were spent on grammar, these last three on the play "Romeo and Juliet." Tom got a kick out of how different students at different times would figure out some of the more explicit passages in Shakespeare's work on their own. They all seemed amazed that someone who lived centuries before them had figured out how hot sex was.

Diesel needed a passing grade in order to eventually graduate. He'd taken and dropped this course twice before and this was the last time he could take it – and he had to pass. He was not at all happy to be at summer school, but it ended up not being too much of an inconvenience to his life-guarding job, and he was really happy to have ended up with Mr. Koehler for a teacher.

Diesel was used to people constantly staring at and appraising him. Everyone had their reasons. Initially, he couldn't figure out what Koehler's were, but the glances were there and since he needed the grade, he went with his gut instincts. They told him to go the tease route.

He sat in the back, usually angling his chair so some part of his body was always exposed to Koehler's line of vision. When everyone was reading or studying on their own, he'd make a point to run his hand over some part of his body, up and down a leg, scratching back and forth along his waistline, rubbing his chest, anything. During discussions, one of his favorite poses was running both hands through his curly blonde hair, locking them behind his head, and slouching in his seat with legs spread. He didn't spend too much time glancing at Koehler; he had to depend on this working on its own.

And then there was the matter of his clothing. Diesel had discovered that he could wear just about anything and look sexy as hell in it. He knew that a lot of gay guys, especially the ones older than he, seemed to like seeing him in tight clothes. That way, they got to see how Diesel's body curved in and bulged out in all the right places. Diesel also liked to tease guys with clothing that showed bits of flesh. And then there was his dick. Diesel knew that his fencepost would be noticed no matter what the covering.

The first week he'd worn his orange life guarding tank top over a pair of loose baggy shorts.

"Swimwear from your job is probably not the most appropriate clothing for school, Diesel, even if it is summer," said Mr. Geary, the advisor assigned to Diesel to counsel him toward graduation. Geary was constantly asking Diesel to make advising appointments with him. Diesel knew it was just because Geary was really hot for him and Diesel had no interest in Geary – other than to tease the fuck out of him. But Diesel didn't want to take too many chances right now, with the three strike rule hanging over him with this class. He decided the issue here was that he was wearing something from work, not the fact that it was a tank top. He stifled the urge to pull it off right then, get into Geary's face and say, "Sorry, Mr. Geary, here it is. What would you like me to be wearing?" But he knew how to get back at Geary.

At his next advising appointment two days later he showed up wearing a skin-tight white tank top with a black stretch short sleeved button down shirt over it, and baggy white painter's pants. He only buttoned two of the middle buttons of the black shirt causing it to stretch out below, framing his bulging abs covered with the white stretched fabric of the tank top, while above the two buttons, the black material caught under the ridge of his massive hanging pecs, accentuating their mass even more. As he walked into Mr. Geary's office, Geary's mouth working to keep from dropping open, Diesel smiled, nodded toward Geary, and then slowly scratched just underneath his left nipple while maintaining eye contact. Diesel was sure that afterwards, Geary had no memory of any "advising" he did that day.

And then of course, there was the effect his clothing had on Koehler. Koehler realized that rules were more relaxed in college. Students stood next to their desks or leaned against the back wall during class if they wanted a break. When Diesel went into one of his stretches at the wall, Koehler just needed to make sure that he was sitting down, and stayed down till his hard-on went away.

Another favorite outfit of Diesel's was a pair of low-rise jeans, tight in the crotch/ass, baggy everywhere else, topped with a cropped football jersey. The jersey would stretch out over Diesel's wide back, shoulders and chest, and fall down like a loose curtain, fluttering against his midsection as he moved.

Koehler was old school when it came to English. He always had his students spending chunks of time working at blackboards. Diesel always volunteered to work at the board on the days he wore his drawstring sweat shorts and a t- shirt. The t-shirt was always too small and rarely reached his waist; the sweat shorts always seemed to be held up by his jutting ass and nothing else. He enjoyed being at the board with his back to Koehler, as Koehler would steal glances at Diesel's exposed lower back. The t-shirt would elevator up and down a few inches as Diesel worked. Though Diesel was hairier than most guys with blonde hair, most of his hair was pretty light colored. One exception was a bushy patch of dark brown hair low on his back along his spine, running into his asscrack. Diesel knew that lots of guys, and some girls, were somehow really turned on by that patch of fur. He had no idea why, but used it because it worked like magic.

Diesel also liked wearing loose khaki pants every once in a while. Never wearing underwear on those days, he loved being able to let the hog "roam free" as he phrased it. He usually wore a wife beater topped with some kind of loose print, maybe Hawaiian, buttoned shirt over it.

On the Wednesday of that last week, Diesel wore his khaki pants. The difference this time was no wife beater. The Hawaiian print shirt was closed with one button. Papers on R&J were due on Friday, same day as the final exam. When the bell rang, the students shuffled out of the class. Koehler looked up to see Diesel getting out of his chair. The one existing button on the shirt caught on the desk's edge and popped off.

"Can I talk to you for a minute, Mr. Koehler?" asked Diesel as he made his way up the aisle of the room, now emptied except for the two of them. With no buttons, the shirt now fluttered open, exposing Diesel's full torso as he made his way to the front. Koehler couldn't take his eyes off of it...remembering Sean's hands and mouth roaming over it.

"Sorry, the button just popped off," said Diesel with a shy smile as he pulled the two sides of his shirt together in front. Diesel waited till he got to the front of the room to do it, watching Koehler's eye feast on his tensed muscles. Diesel stood at the side of the desk, and put his R&J script down on it. "I wanted to ask you about what's going on here in the play," said Diesel, his shirt parting open as he stood.

Koehler was starting to sweat. He sat at the desk, tensed, and stared at the script, not trusting himself to look sideways and see the muscled blond a matter of inches from his face. He could have sworn he felt Diesel's body heat. "What part?" he asked in a pitch a bit higher than normal.

"Right here," Diesel said shoving forward a bit. "I mean all this stuff that Mercutio is saying. I'm not sure I understand all of it. It does sound like he really likes Romeo a lot, but I can't tell if he's happy for Romeo right now. I mean, if they're such good friends, why wouldn't Mercutio be really happy for Romeo? Is there something goin' on that I don't see in these words? Like...like...."

While Diesel talked, Koehler gave into the temptation to glance sideways. He was eye level with Diesel's waist. He saw Diesel's abs rumble against each other as he talked — like a bunch of puppies squirming for a place at a teat. He saw Diesel's treasure trail...dark blonde...thickening till it disappeared into the khaki.

Then. The hog. There it was, swaying in what seemed like slow motion, a pendulum, back and forth, rubbing against the pant's fabric. It moved with the rhythm of Diesel's voice. Koehler could feel precum burping out of his own cockslit. It was all he could do to not moan out loud. Koehler looked up to Diesel's face and gradually remembered that Diesel was talking.

"Like..." said Diesel.

"Like what, Diesel, what do you mean?"

"Well. I know this sounds crazy, but I keep wondering if there's a chance, now don't yell at me and say I'm stupid, but I keep wondering if there's a chance that Mercutio maybe has kinda the hots for Romeo...but can't really talk about it. I mean, did they have gay guys back then, Mr. Koehler?"

"Diesel, there have always been gay men. That lifestyle was treated differently at different times in history. In Ancient Greece, it was an acceptable practice for an older man to have a younger man, sometimes a boy, as a regular sex partner, and be married at the same time."

Diesel put his hands in his front pockets, pulling his pants down slightly. Koehler watched the material shift along the length of the hog. "Wow, that's amazing, Mr. Koehler. Say, I've been working on my paper for this and I was wondering if it would be cheating if I met with you one on one and showed you bits of it. I've got a lot of it done with notes and I'd just like to have the chance to talk to you about it so I'd know if I was on the right track. Could we do that?" Diesel asked with a pleading look.

Koehler was helpless. "Sure, when?"

"I have to run home right now, I can grab my notes. I'm coming back to do some laps in the pool. How about if I meet you here at, let's say, 4?"

"Sounds good to me, Diesel" said Koehler, fighting to keep his breathing under control.

"Thanks a lot, Mr. Koehler, I really really appreciate it!" said Diesel, placing one of his huge hands on Koehler's shoulder. Koehler felt Diesel's body heat almost like a branding iron as he took a sharp breath inward.

"See ya later, Teach!" said Diesel with a smile and a squeeze of Koehler's shoulder, then he jogged out of the classroom. He stopped in the shadows of the hallway and looked through the glass slot of the classroom's back door. A big smile broke out as he watched Koehler jerking in his chair.

As soon as Diesel left the room, Koehler pressed both his balled fists into his crotch. Within seconds his climax erupted. It was Diesel's touch and squeeze that put him over the edge. Had Diesel not left at that exact moment, Koehler knew that he probably would have thrown himself onto Diesel in much the same way that kid Sean had done in the stairwell. Koehler felt ashamed that he desired Diesel so strongly — more strongly than he had desired anyone before.

Koehler actually had to go home and change his messy pants. He raced back to school, getting to his classroom about 10 minutes to

4. Then 4 came and went. Then 4:15. At 4:30, Koehler stormed across campus to the pool. "If that asshole is there, I'm going to ream him," he thought angrily. Though you weren't supposed to enter the pool area in street clothes Koehler stormed in. The pool was empty save for one person doing laps — Diesel. Koehler stood at the shallow end, furious as he watched Diesel swimming away from him, doing the breaststroke. When Diesel reached the far end and made his turn, he spotted Koehler.

"Jesus, I almost gave up on the jackass even showing up!" thought Diesel, "time to notch things up a bit," he continued thinking as he raced toward Koehler. Diesel reached the shallow end of the pool and just about shot out of the water.

"Mr. Koehler, I am SO sorry. I completely lost track of time and believe it or not, was actually thinking about my R&J paper while I was doing laps. Please, please don't be mad at me for this and don't hold it against me. Can we please still meet? I really need your help so I can figure out if I'm heading in the right direction with my paper. Please, Mr. Koehler, please?"

Koehler stood with his arms crossed, tense and angry. He wasn't prepared for the vision in front of him when Diesel came out of the water. Koehler had no idea that Diesel was as muscular as he was now able to see. His blonde locks were plastered to his skull; trails of water ran like ski runs all over Diesel's chiseled frame. Koehler lost any thought of anger when he glanced down at Diesel's crotch. Though he assumed that the water and whatever anxiety would contribute to some kind of dick shrinkage, it was still the biggest piece of meat he'd ever seen in his life. Diesel's red Speedo was filled to the point of bursting. His actual dick pointed downward as well as it could in the suit's pouch. The jump out of the water caused enough suction of the material that his crotch looked shrink-wrapped — the ridge of Diesel's dickhead was so clearly outlined that Koehler could see its shadow on the red material. The strings hadn't been tied and each end hung on either side of the dick. Koehler suddenly thought of the mantube as a north/south continental divide with each string representing the rivers that flowed either to the east or to the west of that mountain range of a cock.

Koehler looked back up to Diesel's damp face. His mouth was slightly open, trails of water continued to move south, a few ran into Diesel's mouth. Diesel stared at Koehler in a pleading way.

"OK, but I don't have a lot of time. Let's hurry," said Koehler, realizing he was giving in to a temptation that he shouldn't give in to.

They walked into the locker room together. Diesel ran into the shower area, talking a mile a minute, apologizing over and over. Koehler stopped listening and sat down on one of the benches by the lockers just outside the shower room. Diesel kept talking even after he turned the shower on. A minute later, a red blur flew across Koehler's line of sight. It was the Speedo. It landed with a thud on a metal ledge. Diesel had tossed them out. Koehler stared at them. A third of the suit was hanging off the ledge, water dripped to the floor. He kept thinking about how it had just been wrapped around Diesel's hard ass and huge cock. He wanted to touch it. As he was about to reach out, the shower flow stopped. Diesel stepped out wearing a towel around his waist, drying himself off quickly with another, still rambling on.

"Diesel, enough apologizing. You screwed up. Let's just get back upstairs to the classroom where we can get some work done. OK?"

"Sure, Mr. Koehler, sure," said Diesel as he tossed aside the towel he'd been drying himself with, and unhooked the other towel from his waist. Facing Koehler, neither speaking, Diesel reached in his locker, brought out a beat up old jockstrap and slowly pulled it on, adjusting his cock and balls in the stretched pouch. Koehler could only swallow, the sight of "the hog" burned into his brain. He then put on a pair of drawstring shorts, a wife beater, and a button down short sleeve shirt over that, leaving it unbuttoned. Koehler led the way back to the classroom.

They ended up talking for almost an hour. Koehler was impressed with the line of logic that Diesel had come up with for his paper. He wanted to present the hypothesis that had Mercutio lived, he would have eventually ended up sharing a household with Romeo and

Juliet. Or, if Romeo had also survived, but not Juliet, then Mercutio and Romeo would have hooked up. Diesel and Koehler sat next to each other in two of the classroom chairs. Diesel used his hands a lot while talking, often touching Koehler when making a point. As before, each touch felt hot on Koehler's skin.

That night at home, Koehler got himself hard remembering a party he'd gone to in college where he ended up fucking 3 women in a little over an hour. It was a sweet time and Koehler could always use that to bring him back from any daydreaming while he was fucking some other woman, including his wife. But this time, instead of seeing the women, different parts of Diesel would float into his mind. Koehler stopped masturbating, telling himself that he'd not beat off again till he could do it with images of women in his head.

Thursday was a low-rise jeans day for Diesel. Since it was the day before the final exam and when papers were due, Koehler spent the class working with people individually as they requested help. Diesel spent the class writing and shifting in his seat, every once in a while getting up for a stretch. Koehler forced his eyes to not watch during the stretches.

Friday morning, Koehler woke up with a jerk, breathing hard, and in a heavy sweat. He had kicked the sheet completely off the bed, realized he was covered with his own cum, and that his asshole felt odd. A wet dream — Diesel. Koehler jumped out of the damp bed and into the shower. The warm stream of liquid helped him relax his muscles. Snippets from the dream bubbled to the surface.

Diesel was standing there dressed as Koehler had never seen him — black leather. Some kind of boots that came up to his mid-thigh, a vest covering his shoulders and upper chest, and a pair of skin tight gloves — nothing else.

There was something in the air that was really different. Diesel kept asking if he looked OK. Koehler backhanded Diesel really hard, realizing at that moment that he was also naked except for a pair of black gauntlet gloves. Diesel brought his hands up to his face, held back tears, and started apologizing. For what, Koehler had no idea.

All he knew was that in this dream, Diesel was being completely subservient to him — and he really liked the way that felt.

He slapped Diesel's huge hanging dick and yelled at him to stop whimpering. Diesel stopped. He started pulling on Diesel's dick, yanking it downward, ordering Diesel to get hard. It wasn't happening fast enough for Koehler; he moved behind Diesel, took off one of his gloves, and started working his fingers into Diesel's ass, all the while yelling at him to get hard. Without too much effort he got his whole fist up Diesel's asshole. He began thrusting into Diesel's ass, punctuating each punch with a yell of "Hard!" He reached around and smiled as he felt the hot hard pole.

Koehler yanked his fist out of Diesel's ass and turned him around, ordering him to take his vest off. Koehler got down on the floor on his back and ordered Diesel to fuck him. Diesel leaned over saying he didn't want to hurt Koehler. Koehler reached up and grabbed a nipple in each hand, pulled and twisted them as hard as he could, and gave his order again. Diesel complied.

Though Koehler had never had anything up his butt his whole life (minus doctor visits), his mind remembered the feel of Diesel's dick going in and out of his ass as a full and tingly feeling. He also remembered that as Diesel held himself over Koehler, he fucked Koehler as if he were doing push ups. Koehler began punching both of Diesel's pecs as they hung above his face like water balloons. He kept yelling for Diesel to go faster and deeper. That's all he could remember of the dream.

As he grabbed the shampoo, he noticed how dirty a few of his fingernails were on his right hand. The nails on his left hand were clean as a whistle. "What the...," said Koehler as he started examining the dirty fingernails under the shower head. "Holy fuck!" Koehler yelled as he realized the dirt under his nails was his own shit! He must have been shoving his fingers up his ass during the wet dream as if it had been Diesel fucking him. That explained why his ass was feeling funny. It also made him pray for the end of that day — the last day of summer classes at Texas A&M – the last day he'd have to see Diesel.

14

Last day of class was always a bit bittersweet. People seemed to have mixed feelings. The students turned in their papers as they arrived and sat down to take the test. Each student said their good-bye as they handed in their test. Diesel chose to wear the same chinos and t-shirt he wore that day Koehler spied on him in the hallway. Koehler kept seeing the t-shirt pulled back over Diesel's head. This time he also kept seeing Diesel's face twisted in ecstasy, as if in the middle of cumming.

"I really appreciate all the extra help you gave me, Mr. Koehler, and again, I'm really sorry I screwed up on the time on Wednesday. That talk straightened out a lot of things in my mind. Believe it or not, I really enjoyed this class...hope you like my paper," said Diesel as he handed in his test. He walked back to his desk in the back of the room to pick up his stuff then walked back up the aisle. Koehler couldn't help but stare at Diesel's cock as it swayed underneath the loose material of his pants.

"See ya," said Diesel with a wink as he walked by the desk and out the door. Koehler gave a long sigh and busied himself straightening the papers on his desk.

Koehler started grading the tests and papers that night. He was determined to finish that quickly, and did so by mid-afternoon on Saturday. Though Diesel did miserably on the test, his paper was actually pretty well thought out. Combined with the mediocre work Diesel did in the first half of the class, Koehler ended up assigning him a C+.

That night he decided to celebrate a few things — the end of the summer session, finishing up all his grading (he'd entered them on a spreadsheet on his computer but decided to wait till Sunday to send them in), and most of all, his ability to resist Diesel. Minor as some might view it, his celebration consisted of ordering a pizza, and enjoying it with beer, and a DVD from Blockbuster.

A couple of minutes after the pizza guy left, Koehler's bell rang again. He ran to the door and opened in, expecting it to be the pizza guy about something, and discovered Diesel.

"Hi, Mr. Koehler. I hope you don't think I'm stalking you or anything; I just really wanted to tell you how much I got out of your class. You're a really good teacher and I wanted to tell you that. I honestly don't care what grade you gave me...really. Well, sorry to bother you. Maybe I'll see you around," he turned to go.

Koehler was pretty shocked to see Diesel. Half the shock was how Diesel looked. He wore a long sleeve silk pullover t-shirt that was a shade of blue that seemed to match his eyes exactly. The shirt fit him like a glove, stretched especially tight over his biceps, chest and the bumps of his abs. But the real shocker was the pants. Black leather. The t-shirt was tucked into Diesel's narrow waist. His crotch pressed obscenely against the buttoned fly. It looked like a dam about to burst. When Diesel turned to go and Koehler gazed on his broad muscled back with that smooth layer of blue covering it, zooming down to an ass that if anything, pressed against the leather more fiercely than in front, Koehler said, unable to stop himself, "Diesel, wait."

Diesel turned back toward Koehler, a hand in each front pocket.

"I'm very glad you liked the class, Diesel. Teachers always like it when that happens. Sorry if I'm a bit flustered, I just didn't expect it to be you...I thought it was the pizza delivery kid coming back with some kind of problem."

"I'm sorry, Mr. Koehler, didn't know you had company. See ya." Diesel turned back around.

"Wait! I don't have any company. Truth is I'm just doin' a little celebrating by myself of the end of the summer. C'mon in for a while. Have a piece of pizza. I'll never finish the whole thing myself," said Koehler, going against all reason. He knew he should just let Diesel walk, but he needed to feast his eyes on Diesel some more. He'd had a couple of beers and didn't realize his clarity was a bit fogged.

"No, I should go."

"Get in here and stop acting stupid," said Koehler as he grabbed Diesel's forearm. The silk material was smooth and Koehler felt Diesel's muscles move underneath it. "I'll never finish the pizza! And all the grading is done. You won't be able to talk me into giving you more than you deserved," Koehler said with a laugh.

"Have a seat," said Koehler as he shut the front door and watched Diesel's hard ass move across the room toward the TV. "Can I get you a Coke?"

"Sure, that would be fine."

"Why are you so dressed up, Diesel?"

Diesel laughed. "Believe it or not, I'm celebrating the end of summer too," he said, stopping and turning to flash a toothy grin toward Koehler. "I was actually on my way to a movie at Cherry Creek Mall. I like dressing up every once in a while. These pants were a gift from a guy I did some work for. I don't own much leather. Too expensive. The shirt is new. But maybe this is all a bit much. What do you think?" asked Diesel as he did a slow turnaround.

"I think you look just fine, Diesel," said Koehler as he watched Diesel rotating in the middle of the room. Not only was he turned on by the sight of Diesel, even the sound of the creaking leather as Diesel turned was getting him hot.

Koehler returned with a Coke for Diesel and a beer for himself, the pizza box still unopened on the coffee table in front of them. "Pardon my manners...I'll grab some napkins, go ahead and dig in," said Koehler as he turned to go back to the kitchen. Diesel decided he'd be more comfortable on the floor so he slid off the couch, leaning his back on it, facing the coffee table and TV.

Two more beers later, another coke for Diesel, and 2/3 of the pizza gone, the 2 of them looked more like two friends having a good time, rather than teacher and student. Sitting on the couch, the bottom part of Koehler's leg rested along Diesel's arm, as Diesel rested while sitting on the floor. Koehler knew he was a bit drunk, but fought to remain clearheaded. He resisted the urge to run his fingers through Diesel's blonde curls. He loved being able to sit back and stare at the back of Diesel's head and see his leather covered legs stretched out underneath the coffee table.

"Hey, Diesel, you ever do any modeling or bodybuilding stuff?"

Diesel cocked his head sideways looking up at Koehler. "Actually, I've done a bit of both, nothing serious though. I know I'd never go far as a model because I'm too bulky. For a guy to make it as a model, he needs to be thinner than I am. And I don't think I'm big enough to compete as a bodybuilder...at least seriously."

"I think you'd make a great model. With a build like yours, you could have a very good career...just depends on what you'd model. And you're plenty big for bodybuilding...plenty," said Koehler as he placed his hand on Diesel's shoulder gently rubbing it. Koehler felt Diesel relax against his leg.

"You got a routine?" asked Koehler.

"What do you mean 'routine'?"

"Bodybuilding, goof!" said Koehler lightly slapping the back of Diesel's head.

"No. I don't really know what to do. But I have watched a lot of competitions on TV and I've taped them and then play them back trying to copy some of the guys."

Koehler's mind filled with images of Diesel in a tiny posing strap unable to contain his cock and balls, a darkly tanned body, smeared with a thick coat of oil reflecting the bright lights. For Koehler's purposes, all Diesel would need to do would be to stand there, nothing more.

"Show me."

"What?"

"C'mon. Show me some kind of posing routine. I'll be the judge. C'mon...for laughs," said Koehler as he got off the couch and tried to lift Diesel, who got up and walked around the couch.

"Over there in the middle of the room where there's some space. Yeah, there. OK. Audience is this way," said Koehler as he knelt on the couch facing away from the TV toward Diesel.

"I don't think I can do this. I feel kind of stupid," said Diesel with his arms at his sides.

"Oh, c'mon," Koehler pleaded, "just imagine you're on a stage with lots of lights. There's a panel of judges watching you carefully and a crowd of fans screaming their support."

"Well, OK, but I don't want to rip this," said Diesel as he first unbuttoned the top of his pants, pulled off the silk t-shirt, and tossed it to Koehler. "Guard this," he said with a smile.

Diesel started his routine. Actually he had a few of them. The one he did now was a version of the one he did for private clients. He got paid good money for doing this elsewhere, but on the line now was his grade. Besides, Diesel loved that feeling of power over guys when they got completely mesmerized by his body. Since his legs were covered, he focused most of his movements on his upper body and arms, but kept in mind that some guys, and he suspected Koehler was one, got off on leather and muscles. He made sure to work in a few moves that showed his leg muscles wrestling underneath the leather.

Koehler was entranced. He immediately went hard and unconsciously started pressing his dick into the couch. He'd never been to a bodybuilding competition, but what this guy was doing was amazing. Koehler loved the way Diesel was making different parts of his chest expand and retract. And those arms! From the elbow down they looked like bars of different size steel lying next to each other under the skin. From the elbow up they were just one bulge building onto the next.

Diesel turned around. Koehler had to get closer. He dropped the t-shirt, stepped over the couch and moved toward the musclegod. Diesel's back formed a "V" covered with mounds of moving muscle. His arms moved like they were sides of beef attached to his shoulders. A sheen of sweat glistened on Diesel's skin — and on Koehler's face. Koehler moved closer. He was taking deep deep breaths.

"Can I...," Koehler whispered questioningly.

"Sure, I don't bite...too hard," said Diesel, still with his back to Koehler.

Koehler placed both palms on Diesel's back. As Diesel kept moving in his posing, Koehler was now able to feel the muscles moving. His hands started roaming over the muscled terrain of Diesel's back. Diesel brought a hand down to his crotch, and then turned to face Koehler.

Koehler pulled back, not in fright, but in sheer shock at suddenly being that close to an entirely different musculature. Koehler's eyes first dropped to Diesel's crotch where another button had been popped open. The opening leather now flapped downward on each side and the waist pulled away from Diesel's skin. Diesel's cock and balls were still hidden behind the layer of warm leather, and still advancing their case for release. Koehler followed Diesel's treasure trail upward as it snaked through his abs and disappeared. Above that were the hanging masses of pec flesh with a proud hard nipple at each center. As Diesel continued his sensual dance, their eyes met.

"Can I...," Koehler whispered questioningly.

Diesel just smiled. Koehler fell forward, open mouth landing on a pec, he grabbed the other pec with one hand, kneading it like dough. The other hand cupped one of Diesel's hard ass cheeks. Koehler pulled on the warm leather covering it, jamming his crotch into Diesel's. Diesel put a hand on the back of Koehler's head, helping it travel around his chest. Koehler was mumbling incoherently, saliva ran freely from his mouth. Koehler moved his hand from Diesel's ass to his crotch and looked up at Diesel's face.

"Can I...," Koehler whispered questioningly.

Diesel smiled again and pulled open the rest of the pants' buttons and placed each of Koehler's hands on the waist of his pants and dropped his own hands to his sides. "Your turn."

Koehler dropped to his knees, his arms now bent with his hands resting on the waist of the leather pants on either side, his eyes level with Diesel's basket, the smell of the leather was intoxicating. Koehler pulled. Diesel limited his movements to a slight swaying of his hips. Koehler pulled more and the leather noisily slid downward. Diesel's dick popped out and hit Koehler in the chin. Koehler groaned.

Diesel grabbed the back of Koehler's head holding him about a foot away from his fat red swaying cock. Diesel's balls, freed from their heated cell, moved lazily in their low sack.

"You want it? You want the hog?" asked Diesel in a hoarse whisper.

Koehler was afraid that if he took his eyes off the dick for a second it might disappear. He stared at it, not blinking and nodded his head as well as he could with Diesel's fist having a firm hold in the back.

"Tell me. Tell me what you want, Teach."

"I want the hog, Diesel...I want the hog," Koehler panted.

Koehler reached for it with his hands. Diesel slapped them away. Then Diesel started moving Koehler's head back and forth toward his dick, teasing Koehler by allowing him to get close to his prize, but not able to touch it with his straining mouth or tongue. He then grasped his tube of manmeat and slapped Koehler repeatedly underneath his chin with it.

Diesel pulled Koehler's head back a bit, pointing his cockhead toward Koehler's face. "Hey, Mr. Koehler, the hog has a question he wants to ask."

Koehler looked up at Diesel's face perplexed.

"The hog," said Diesel, looking from Koehler's eyes to his dick.

Koehler looked at the fat red one eyed dickhead staring at him. Diesel slid his fist forward on the length of his cock, grabbing near the tip with his thumb and forefinger.

"What grade did you give Diesel?" said Diesel as he squeezed his piss slit open and shut. Koehler looked back up at Diesel.

"Talk to the hog, Teach!" Koehler's eyes raked down Diesel's muscled body, ending at his dickhead.

"What grade?"

"C"

"What? Diesel deserves better than that, Teach. Can you do better than that? It would make me happy if you did...very happy."

"B"

"Not good enough. Diesel worked really hard in your class...really hard. I like working hard too. Would you like me to work hard?" Diesel started slapping Koehler's face with his huge dick. Koehler knelt in a trance as the warm truncheon jarred his face over and over. Diesel stopped and held his dick about 8 inches from Koehler's face; a burp of precum seeped out of the slit and started its slow journey to the floor.

"Reconsidering?"

"A"

"What?" said Diesel, "the hog can't hear you."

"A"

"Get closer. Tell him again," said Diesel as he pulled Koehler's head to within a few inches of his piss slit. Koehler was aching to get his mouth on the red piece of flesh in front of him.

"A...A...A...," Diesel pulled Koehler's head forward so his dick rammed into Koehler's surprised face. He pulled Koehler's head back. Then forward again. This time Koehler opened his mouth wide and sucked in as much of Diesel's dickhead as he could. He grabbed Diesel's dick with both hands and sucked on the head as if his life depended on it. He pulled off for a moment to take some heaving breaths; gobs of saliva fell out of his mouth. Diesel guided Koehler's mouth back to the tip of his hardening and expanding dick. Koehler latched onto the head, and began pumping the length of it with both hands. It hardened more under his grasp, eventually feeling like wet velvet being rubbed over a steel tube.

"Yes, that's it, Mr. Koehler. Make the hog spit. Hog likes to spit...hog loves your warm mouth and tongue...oh yeah, suuuucccckkkkk...," said Diesel as he shoved his pelvis forward, dropped his head back, and gently rubbed Koehler's head. Suddenly his balls jerked up and both he and Koehler sensed the coming tidal wave.

Waves of cum cannoned out of Diesel's slit. Diesel pulled Koehler's sucking mouth off of his dick after the first couple of volleys; Koehler lost his grip on his prize. Diesel shot the rest all over Koehler's face watching it drip down his neck onto his chest and back. Diesel grabbed his still hard dick and began rubbing it all over Koehler's face, ears and neck, spreading the thick cum. Diesel then pulled the almost comatose Koehler to his feet, locked lips with him, and gave him a passionate kiss, shoving his tongue in Koehler's mouth like an anteater at a feast, while grinding their bodies together. Diesel unlocked their mouths and held his face within inches of Koehler's. They stared at each other, mouths open, panting, eyes locked.

"And Mr. Koehler, when I check my grades online in a few days, if that A becomes an A+, I'll be back and I can show you more posing routines." While talking, Diesel reached around Koehler, grabbed his ass with one hand, slid the other one up and down Koehler's asscrack, and pressed their bodies together. "Lots more...know what I mean?" Diesel let go of Koehler and watched him fall to the ground in a heap.

Diesel grabbed Koehler's t-shirt, ripped it off of him, and used it to clean off his cock. He walked over to the couch, grabbed his own t-shirt, and dropped Koehler's cum stained t-shirt in its place. He walked back to Koehler, lying on the floor, who hadn't taken his eyes off Diesel's sweat covered body. Diesel stood spread-eagled over the prone body so that Koehler looked straight up at him. He pulled his satin t-shirt on, tucked it in, "Hog says bye...for now," said Diesel as he grabbed his cock and stuffed it and his balls back into their leather cage, and buttoned up.

"Remember, Teach, 'A+' and you get more of this," said Diesel as he rubbed his crotch. He walked over to the coffee table, grabbed a piece of cold pizza, and wolfed it down as he walked to the door. Koehler stayed hard as he watched the blue silk clinging to Diesel's wet back.

CHAPTER 2

The Cop

"Fuck, this is all I need!" groaned Diesel as big drops of rain started to fall while he walked down the road. On his way home from the pool, he was dressed in an old t-shirt and sweat shorts with his Speedos underneath. It was a freak storm, came out of nowhere and pummeled Diesel who very quickly was completely soaked. Under other circumstances, he would have been very pleased with the shrink-wrapping his wet clothing did of his massive teen body.

Only after he heard the electronic beep of the state police car did he take notice. It had stopped a little ahead of him; Diesel ran to the open passenger window.

"Want a ride? Nobody should be out in this."

"Thanks a lot, officer!" Diesel yanked the door open and jumped in. "Sorry I'm getting your car all wet...oh shit, my feet are muddy too."

"Don't worry about it, it's only water, there's a towel in the backseat." Diesel sat up and reached over the seat for the towel in the back, exposing his firm midsection to the cop who just happened to be looking in that direction.

"Well, I do really appreciate the ride. I am soaked to the bone, Officer...?" sticking out his hand.

"Gardner, Jacob...Jake."

While shaking hands Diesel started thinking that the day might not end up being a total waste after all — this cop was a looker, chiseled face, brown crewcut, and what looked like the kind of body that should always be the kind you'd want to find inside a uniform, based on his exposed thickly muscled forearms. Diesel had gone to the pool assuming the new hunky lifeguard would be on duty. He purposely didn't wear his swimmer's jock under his Speedos which garnered his package the kind of up front and center attention he liked and it craved. Some would call it obscene, some would call it hot — Diesel was only interested in the latter group. He did some diving, swam around and sunned himself for a few hours — hunk never came on duty —left frustrated.

"You in school,...?"

"Sorry, name's Diesel. Yes, I am, officer, Texas A&M."

"College seems so long ago, though I only graduated 8 years ago. I'm sure it's still boring as ever."

Smelling an opportunity, with a twitch of his dick Diesel replied, "Yeah, I'm sure it is. Stupid classes, stupid tests, stupid rules. Thank god for sports!" Diesel peeled his soaked t-shirt off and dropped it with a plop on the floor in front of his seat, spreading his legs out at the same time. He then rubbed his chest, abs, and arms with the towel. Then he wrapped the towel behind him, leaning back pressing into the back of the seat rubbing back and forth drying both his back and the seatback.

"Yeah, that was the best part of college. What sports do you play?" asked Officer Gardner, taking in Diesel's sculpted body. "Jesus, this kid is built!" went through his mind.

"Swimming, football, and my favorite, wrestling," replied Diesel, flashing a bright smile at the cop. The rain water kept trickling its way from his scalp, down his smooth face and neck, down his mountainous pecs, some making a ski jump off of them, splashing onto his abs and slithering down to his wet shorts.

"I would have guessed from your build either football or wrestling. I played baseball and swam. Put on a few pounds since then but like to tell myself its muscle, not fat."

"You look pretty well put together, officer," replied Diesel, "May I?" as he put the flat of his hand on the officer's waist. "Feels pretty solid to me."

On the one hand Diesel wanted to feed this guy's ego. On the other hand, the guy really seemed to be in good shape. The whole time, Diesel kept doing the rubbing and pressing into the seatback, moving ever so slowly making it look like he wasn't paying attention to what he was doing when what he was actually doing was an erotic lap dance on himself. He could feel his dick slowly unfurl as he aroused himself.

Jake noticed the smooth movements in the corner of his rear view mirror and stole a few sideways glances at the blonde muscle guy, who pretended like he didn't notice. "Shit, I think this guy is coming on to me," ran through his mind.

"You lift weights?"

"Yeah, have for a while now, pretty seriously the last few years," said Diesel. Pulling the towel from behind, he now lifted his ass up off the seat and looked to his right out the window, taking a lot of time to spread the towel underneath him. Of course, this put his ample basket on display for Officer Gardner. Diesel smirked when he caught Jake stealing a glance at his damp crotch.

"If you don't mind my saying, you look pretty solid yourself, and I bet the cheerleaders don't complain."

Diesel sat back down on the towel pulling the ends up to dry the front of his shorts. Again, he pretended to innocently soak up the wetness when what he was actually doing was rhythmically pressing into his crotch causing his biceps to bulge to hardness with the same rhythm.

"You mean my dick? Yeah, I'm pretty proud of it. Only complaint I've ever had about my soldier is that it's a might big."

Jake was surprised by the guy's straightforwardness and changed the subject. "I've got some weights that I use...but I don't really know what I'm doing. What I should do is join a gym. There's one downtown that gives discounts to cops and firemen, but I've already invested in the equipment I have, and I can use it whenever I want.

Diesel responded, "At a gym, you can also get a trainer. It's more money, but worth it because they know how to get results. It's surprising the mistakes guys make while training alone."

By this time, he was employing the same trick of keeping up his pumping/drying motions all around his hips and waist, focusing of course on his crotch, but doing them very slowly. Jake shifted in his seat.

"Sorry, completely forgot to ask, am I heading in the right direction? I'm nearing the end of my shift and am actually heading toward my place without thinking. Where should I take you?"

Diesel thought, "Buddy, it's where I'm gonna take you!" but said, "I live in this direction too, don't worry. So what kind of weights do you have?"

"Actually just some free weights, barbells, a rack and an adjustable bench, nothing fancy, but you don't make a lot in your earlier years as a public servant," Jake glanced at Diesel with a smile. Diesel was waiting for the eye contact anc at the same moment pressed into his crotch with the towel releasing a breath and jutting his chin forward ever so slightly in response. Again, Jake shifted. Diesel could see the worm dangling on the hook in front of Jake's flushed face.

"So what did you mean about guys making mistakes training?"

"I've picked up a few things from my coaches over the years, and from some other older guys. I guess one common mistake is that guys tend to think the more weight they use, the better. Truth is it's better to use a slightly lighter weight but just go through the motion, the full motion, slowly and deliberately. It's not how many reps you can do, its how many you can do in good form."

"No shit? Really? I seem to work hard witn the weights but I'm not putting on muscle the way I think I should."

"Could be a number of things you're doing wrong. And then there are some easy 'right' things you could start doing."

"Diesel, would you mind coming over to my place sometime and giving me some pointers? I'd pay you what you think its worth, or feed you, or something — you name it. I don't think I need a full time trainer, just someone to point me in the right direction."

"Tell ya what, officer. You said you're near the end of your shift, right? I don't have to be home for hours. Let's go to your place now. I'll look at the routine you follow, give whatever help I can, and you then feed me. Sound like a plan?"

"That would be awesome, Diesel! And please, call me Jake."

The rain eased up by the time they got to Jake's condo. Jake seemed a bit nervous...like he wasn't used to having people over. Diesel saw that the weight equipment was spread out in what was the dining room area.

"Guess you don't do much entertaining, huh?"

"Never had a need for a dining room set...it's only me. Besides, where else would the weights go?"

"Do you stretch before you train, Jake?"

"No, why?"

"Shame on you, officer! Stretching loosens the muscles and decreases the possibility of straining one while working out."

Diesel took off his still damp shorts, and laid them along with his t-shirt on a stool by the front door. He started doing some slow stretches in his Speedos.

"C'mon, get comfortable, Jake...and stretch."

Jake quickly removed his uniform and got down to a jockstrap. He tried his best to mimic Diesel's moves. "Interesting," thought Diesel, "a jock instead of underwear or going cammo, wouldn't have guessed that, and it doesn't look all that fresh." Diesel also liked the fact that Jake was hairier than he suspected. Nice spread of fur on his chest, legs hairier than you'd think, and an interesting patch of hair low on his back just above the ass, the same as Diesel, which he found very arousing.

"OK, that's enough. Pick up a couple of the 5 pound barbells and let me see you do some curls."

Jake obediently picked up the barbells and started pumping.

"Slower, Jake...even slower. Look at your right fist as it comes up and then goes down. Focus on it. See the smooth arc that it's making...follow it back and forth. OK, same with left fist. Keep doing both of them, but look at and focus on the left one. See the arc. You're picking up speed, slow down...or I'll have to give you a ticket!"

Diesel let Jake work for a few minutes on his own. "OK, stop. What went through your head while you were doing that?"

"It was incredible, Diesel! I really did start to visualize that arc of movement. And I felt like I was putting all my energy into my fist. I could feel the bicep and the tricep expanding and contracting. And..."

"What?"

"Well, I feel stupid, but I think it was starting to get me a bit excited. Why would that happen? I feel so dumb even saying it."

"That's natural, Jake, happens all the time. It's a primal thing. You're focusing on your body, working your muscles, getting all sweaty, pulse rises, breathing deepens. Sometimes when I work out, I'm so hard at the end of a set, that I have to force myself not to take a break and beat off, and sometimes I do anyway!

OK, this next one will work arms and abs. Sit sideways on the bench facing the wall mirror so you can see what you're doing. Now lean back into me...it's OK, I'm here, you won't fall."

Jake leaned back slowly, Diesel had squatted down, Jake's head landed on Diesel's firm left pec. The skin felt really warm.

"Now lift your legs just off the ground and start doing slow curls again. Right! You got it. Keep going."

Though they were almost naked, the air was still pretty humid from the rainfall and by now both guys were sweating quite a bit. Diesel squatted a bit more so that his head was now next to Jake's — his mouth breathing in and out next to Jake's right ear. Diesel reached around each side of Jake under his arms and started caressing Jake's abs.

"Focus on the arm movement. Look at your fuckin' abs! You are in great shape, man."

Jake got hard instantly. He couldn't help it with Diesel rubbing his abs and breathing hot air next to his ear.

31

"I don't know what you're doing right now, Diesel...I'm not gay or anything...besides, you're young, just a college kid" said Jake as his eyes locked on Diesel's in the mirror.

Diesel let his hands slide off of Jake's body and slowly stood up, never breaking eye contact, till he was standing straight up. His basket ended up in the same place his head had just been...on top of Jake's right shoulder, pressing against Jake's ear. He slowly raised his arms into a double bicep pose.

"I didn't say you were gay, Jake. I'm just someone who likes people who keep in shape, and I like showing that appreciation. And does this look like the body of 'just a college kid'? As far as what I'm doing right now, I'm helping you get an even better body."

Diesel held the pose as Jake continued the curls. They broke eye contact at the same moment and shifted their gaze to Diesel's crotch in the mirror. Diesel's dick was so huge that as it started to fill out in the Speedo, it looked like there was a small animal inside shifting in its sleep.

Diesel shifted again moving his dick to the back of Jake's head, reached forward, brought his arms down and started rubbing Jake's abs some more. Jake gave in to it. He was starting to lose focus as low groans forced their way out of his throat. Diesel's hands moved up to Jake's firm succulent pecs and started caressing them, gently tugging on the nipples.

"That's it, Jake. Focus on how your muscles feel as they expand and contract. Slow...go slow."

Diesel stood up with his hands resting on Jake's shoulders. The Speedos were a size too small and were no match for Diesel's soldier as it worked its way out of the top of the Speedos. He began gently thrusting against the back of Jake's head. The short bristly brown hairs tickled Diesel's naked dick and got him even hotter. Jake let the dumbbells fall out of his hands, let his arms and legs drop, and let his head move with Diesel's pumps as he watched what was happening in the mirror in front of him through half closed eyelids.

Diesel was a leaker...and he was proud of it. By now, he had pumped out enough precum to have changed Jake's prickly hair to something more like a bed of warm pasta. He wanted to get off and grabbed Jake's head by the jaws to hold it in place as he rubbed it harder and faster.

"Oh, yeah, Jake...yeah. Look at me, Jake look at my sweaty body getting all hot for you."

Jake looked at their reflection. Diesel's body was fully pumped, abs tightening with each thrust, arms tensed holding Jake's head, those massive pecs shuddering in waves with each hit.

"My dick, Jake, my dick. See it? See it pop up over your head? See it leakin' juice? That's all for you, Jake...you...you...you...," Diesel continued with each thrust.

Jake reached back and grabbed the back of each of Diesel's thighs. He was hypnotized watching Diesel's angry red helmet jack up into sight and then quickly retreat, over and over, sometimes fast, sometimes agonizingly slow. He pulled on Diesel's legs while his slack mouth moaned incoherently.

"Yeah, Jakey, yeah, almost there... " Diesel let his head fall back slightly as he approached release, rocking it back and forth. The few blonde strands not plastered to his head with sweat, launched drops of it outward. He suddenly grabbed Jake's head with such force that it was lucky for Jake that he was so relaxed and out of it. Diesel rammed upward on Jake's head with his dick and watched the first spurt of cum fly into the air. Four more forceful shots followed, each accompanied with a grunting, "Huhhuunnn!" from Diesel.

After a few seconds Diesel came back down to earth...he surveyed his work. As always, cum seemed to be everywhere. Diesel's soldier turned into a fireman when it came to climax time and pumped cum out like it was trying to put out a fire. The first shot had gone up a few feet in the air, arcing forward, and landed with a splat on the wooden floor in front of the mirror. The other three marked Jake — one hit his left thigh, one the top of his jockstrap, and the third landed on Jake's right cheek and was now making its way over his jaw and down his neck.

Of course Diesel's flow hadn't stopped with the major eruptions. Like an earthquake, Diesel always sent aftershocks. One landed on the bridge of Jake's nose and treated it like the continental divide, running evenly down toward each corner of Jake's mouth. The last of it spread out over Jake's forehead running into his hair and ears. Diesel was still lightly thrusting against Jake's head...cum continued to drool out of his slit, into Jake's hair. Diesel felt like he was rubbing a warm melting slab of chocolate.

"Help...me...Diesel...help...," panted Jake.

It was then that Diesel realized that Jake hadn't cum. His hard-on stood like a steel beam and pulled the worn jock away from his body. A silver dollar sized dollop of precum seeped through the jock.

Diesel quickly pulled up one end of the weight bench, locking it up at a 45 degree angle, swung Jake around so he was sitting correctly on the bench, pushed Jake's chest backward till his back slapped against the raised part of the bench, and then wrapped an arm around each of Jake's calves pulling him forward so his ass balanced on the end of the bench. Jake's torso slid down the back of the bench as he was pulled forward...the pulling stopped when Jake's head was the only part still angled upward. Jake didn't even notice.

Diesel brought his face toward Jake's crotch and stuck his tongue into the mass of dark pubic hair puffed out of the jockstrap. Jake's balls were already pulled up tight. As Diesel suspected...he was ready to blow.

"Like this?" Diesel asked as he grabbed the middle of Jake's shaft with his open mouth and hummed through the fabric of the jockstrap.

"How `bout this?" following with doing the same to Jake's dickhead, as Jake's slightly sweet precum mixed with Diesel's saliva.

"Uummmmgggghhhhh…aaagggggghhhhhh…uuuuggggghhhh…." was all Jake was capable of producing.

Diesel stood up suddenly, ripped the old jockstrap off Jake and pulled off his own Speedo. He tossed the jockstrap toward the living room, balled up the cum and sweat stained Speedos, and crammed them into Jake's mouth. He squatted again and grabbed Jake's dick with his right fist.

"Look at me, Jake. You're gonna want to watch this," as Diesel began a slow caress of Jake's dick. He didn't want to jack it just yet…just squeeze it a few times like a ripe cantaloupe. His left hand started a rub back and forth from Jake's shriveled up ball sack, past his pucker, and then back again.

"You're a hairy fucker back here, Jake. Did you know that?"

Jake just stared at Diesel's face, cheeks puffed out, stuffed with the Speedos, sweat dripping off his cop body.

Diesel saw a look in Jake's eyes he'd seen in many other men… raw animal desire…pleading…begging. Now it was just Diesel's index finger sliding through the forest of wet butt hair, then just circling around Jake's hole. He could feel the hole contracting and switched the dick squeezing to a twisting motion. Diesel waited for a signal. Jake's muffled scream coincided with his dick tensing. Diesel rammed his finger into Jake's asshole. The cop's dick went off like a machine gun spraying giant spurts of cum in all different directions. Diesel's favorite part of these exercises was feeling the guy's ass sucking on his finger…always got him excited.

Diesel stood up, rested his hands on his hips, his huge dick angling outward. "Well, would you look at that? You shot your cannon all over the place…even got some on my dick! Now I didn't ask you to do that, and I think that was pretty forward of you. What say you clean it off?"

Diesel spread his muscular legs and started walking toward Jake's head, one leg on either side of Jake's body as it rested on the weight bench. Diesel sat down, ass to dick. Jake's still swollen dick had been resting on his abs. Diesel's asscrack now covered it like a tunnel. Their eyes locked, Diesel started squeezing his ass cheeks while Jake started an upward fucking motion in response.

Jake's arms came up as if on their own and grabbed Diesel's waist pressing him more in his dick. Diesel pulled the Speedos out of Jake's mouth, tossed them aside, and started wiping his remaining cum off of Jake's face. There were a few gobs of it that Diesel let hang from his fingers above Jake's open panting mouth. Diesel chuckled as he lowered his hand to Jake's mouth and watched Jake feverishly suck his fingers.

"But what about my little soldier? He can't stand up proud for his country with your cum on him? Can he? Help this soldier, Jake, help him."

Diesel scooted forward, freeing Jake's dick. Only then did Jake actually really look at what was in front of his eyes...a huge dick... with an even larger mushroom head that had a ridge around it that must have stuck out over a quarter of an inch. It looked like a cannon with a huge helmet on top. His eyes widened with fear as Diesel slid slowly forward.

"Yeah...now you know why I call him my little soldier. He wears his helmet proudly. C'mon, clean him up like a good officer of the law. And remember, he doesn't like any sharp objects touching him so if I feel any teeth, you won't be in shape to make any arrests for quite a while."

Diesel scooted forward again, his dickhead slapped at Jake's lower lip. Fear and shock kept Jake from saying anything. His eyes shot back and forth between Diesel's eyes and Diesel's dick — eyes — dick — eyes — dick — everything started to look hot and needy.

"C,mon, officer...tongue?"

Jake's tongue touched Diesel's dickhead. As he pulled back his tongue, Diesel scooted forward so that half his sizable helmet was in Jake's mouth, the top of it pressing against Jake's upper teeth.

Diesel reached down and gently rubbed the side of Jake's head. "Remember what I said about teeth, Jake."

Jake opened his mouth wider...Diesel slid in further. "Tell you what, Jake. I'll get the whole head in, you wash your tongue around it, I'll pull out and we'll call it even. K?" Diesel pushed forward and felt his dickhead's rim work past Jake's lips.

Jake realized he couldn't breathe and started to panic. "Breath through your nose, Jake, your nose. Calm down...now, the tongue," Diesel was now caressing Jake's head with both hands. He felt the tongue working its way around his helmet and tossed his head backwards in delight.

"Oh, Jakey, you are gooooood at this...real good. Keep moving... yes...like that." Diesel shoved another inch into Jake's mouth. Jake jerked his head, as well as he could, and started to panic again as a choke rose up in his throat. "Stop it!" Diesel slapped Jake's face really hard, "stop being a wuss." Diesel shoved in another inch. Jake's face went beet red as he choked more fiercely.

Diesel pulled his dick out of Jake's mouth and brought his face down to Jake's. Sweat dripped off his face onto Jake's. "You're gonna do this, Jake. You can do it. I want you to do it...and you want to do it...trust me."

Before Jake could react, Diesel shoved his dick back into Jake's mouth. He grabbed Jake's head and started fucking it. Jake realized he had nowhere to go and the only thing he could do was hit Diesel with his fists, which he did. But Diesel had the advantage. Jake was on his back, Diesel had all his weight on Jake. Jake stopped hitting Diesel when he realized that he'd better focus on being able to breathe, which at the moment he couldn't.

"Oh, mama! You are good! Take me to heaven, Jakey, let me hear the angels sing!" as Diesel pumped faster and deeper into Jake's mouth. This never took Diesel long, and only a couple of the other guys in the past had ever passed out. He wondered if Jake would be another one.

Jake was frantic. Not only could he not breath out of his nose, but snot started shooting out of it instead of air. He started to see stars when he suddenly felt Diesel's dick expand in his mouth and throat.

"Aaaaaaahhhhhh!" bellowed Diesel as he pulled Jake's head into his pubic hair and pulsed his load down that warm wet tunnel. He pulled out quickly after two pumps and let the rest spray on Jake's face. Jake choked and coughed, saliva sprayed out of his mouth, a combination of cum and snot bubbled out of his nostrils.

Diesel stood up towering over the heaving cop. Panting, he said, "Thanks for picking me up, Officer Gardner. You're a credit to your department. I'll see myself out. If you ever want to get together again, think about coming to one of my wrestling meets at school. I could show some different holds."

Diesel sauntered toward the front door. Even in his current stupor, Jake loved Diesel's look from behind — massive shoulders narrowing to a firm small waste, a bubble butt that churned as Diesel walked, and legs like a colossus. Jake reached the front door, and bent down to grab his shorts and t-shirt. Just before opening the door, he turned around to the still recovering Jake, flashed him that perfect white toothed smile, a few strands of curly blonde hair bounced on his forehead. Diesel grabbed his dick with one hand flopping it up and down toward Jake, "Bye, bye, officer." He then pulled on his shorts, threw the t-shirt over his shoulder and walked out the door.

CHAPTER 3

The Younger Wrestler

"Aaarrrggghhh!" Diesel grunted out as he eased back after his tenth rep of the third set he was doing on the pec deck. He'd been working out in his college weight room for almost an hour moving from machine to machine and was both pretty pumped up and pretty tired. He'd removed his shirt before mounting the pec deck, glancing over at the kid as he threw the shirt behind the machine.

Danny Adams had been in the weight room also for the last half hour, shadowing Diesel on the machines. At the moment he was on the mats doing some push ups. He was in awe of Diesel's body and his hard-on had been aching for the past ten minutes. Watching Diesel tour the weight machines in his tank top, black nylon shorts and lace up boots was just too much for Danny. He hadn't joined the wrestling team till his junior year, thinking he was too small, but he'd always wanted to wrestle. He'd been going to the Texas A&M wrestling meets since freshman year, mainly to watch Diesel dominate the field. Danny was the smallest senior on the team at and at about 5'7" and 145 pounds. He believed his best feature was his incredible bubble butt that lots of people noticed, lots of ass grabbing with more than a few cases of people, mainly older men, finding ways to touch or rub against it in public. But he was in awe of the sheer muscular mass of Diesel.

When Diesel took off his tank top and revealed his incredible torso, dripping with sweat, Danny had to actually look away for a minute and stop his push ups — he knew that he might pass out otherwise. After Diesel's second set on the pec deck, he had rested for about a full minute, breathing heavily with his eyes closed. He flexed his pecs a few times knowing that Danny was probably watching. Danny's jaw dropped watching them tense, relax and ripple seductively. At the end of his third set, Diesel dropped his arms to his side, and stared at Danny with a glazed over look while taking deep breaths.

Danny ran to the locker room, locked himself in a stall, yanked down his gym shorts and jock, and grabbed his aching cock. Images of Diesel's body pressing on his, Diesel licking his ears, sucking on his neck, rubbing his muscles all over Danny, Diesel caressing Danny's butt, flooded his mind. "Uuugggghhh!" squeaked out of Danny's mouth as his cock snot splattered onto the stall door. He heard the locker room door open, hurriedly grabbed some toilet paper, sloppily wiped up his mess, threw it in the toilet, flushed, attempted to straighten his gym clothes, and opened the door.

Diesel opened a locker three down from Danny's, dropped his shirt onto the bench and pulled his gym bag out quickly. He glanced over at Danny as he walked out of the stall, "Hey, kid, how ya doin'?"

"Fine," Danny whispered as he opened his locker shaking a bit, realizing that the guy he'd just cum over was right next to him. Diesel was still breathing heavily from his workout; a sheen of sweat covered his muscles. Veins popped out all over his body as his heart pumped blood throughout his system. He quickly unlaced his boots and threw them in his bag. He pulled his shorts off, quickly followed by his jock, grabbed a towel and started rubbing himself all over.

"Don't tell anyone I didn't take a shower, 'kay, kid?" he smiled at Danny. Danny dropped down straddling the bench, knowing he'd faint otherwise.

"I'm late for a photo session," said Diesel as he began to towel dry his sweat soaked blonde curls. The towel covered his face and Danny took the chance to drink in the sight. Diesel's dick was the largest one Danny had ever seen — as long as it was wide, marbled with veins, and topped with a perfectly shaped huge helmet of a head. The whole monster swayed gently as Diesel rubbed his hair. Danny could have sworn it was causing a slight breeze, sending a whiff of Diesel's musky odor toward him.

Diesel was having a field day. He'd seen that look on lots of guys in the past — never knew when it was more jealousy or lust, and didn't really care. He'd known Danny all through college, but wasn't attracted to twinks. But Danny also had a butt on him that Diesel now ached to get to know — that combined with his short white blonde buzz cut and chocolate brown eyes made Diesel want him even more. Though both were seniors, the fact that Diesel was a year older and much larger, everywhere, than Danny, had caused them to develop a relationship where Danny was the "kid".

Danny always wore a loose fitting size small singlet, but one that always tautly stretched across his pert erect butt. Diesel decided it was time to bust this cherry. He ached to have his monster cock jammed into that tiny round butt, pumping a load of hot jism as far as he could into the kid's chute.

Diesel turned back to his locker to grab some clothes. Danny's eyes widened as he noticed how Diesel's back muscles swooped downward to what looked liked an impossibly narrow waist, and then burst outward over a mammoth ass that looked hard enough to take a bite out of.

Diesel pulled on a pair of shorts, "Oh my God," thought Danny, "he's not gonna wear any underwear!" He crammed his upper body into a tight white t-shirt with a Superman logo on it which stopped about an inch above the waist of his shorts, and grabbed his gym bag.

"See ya round, squirt!" said Diesel as he squeezed by Danny, giving him a rub on the scalp. Diesel's crotch briefly touched Danny's shoulder and he felt that monster cock slam his shoulder like a pendulum. Diesel smirked as he turned around just before leaving the locker room, noticing that Danny hadn't moved — like he was frozen or something.

Danny sat staring a few feet ahead on the bench. Jock. Soaked used worn jock. Diesel's stretched out jockstrap sat on the bench. Danny just stared at it, imagining he could see steam rising. Finally he reached for it, grabbed it in a trembling fist, and raised it to his face surprised as how dense it felt. He took a long sniff. His hot breath came out in a moan into the jock's damp material as he reacted to the heady odor. He dropped the jockstrap downward and began rubbing it on his chest. Danny ran to the shower room, ripped off his shorts and jockstrap, and began rubbing Diesel's jockstrap all over his hardened dick. He then reached around and started rubbing his ass with the jockstrap while frantically yanking his dick with the other hand.

"Dee...Dee...Dee...," he breathed saying each word as he swiped along his asscrack, now mixing his own sweat with Diesel's. Danny started to lose his balance in his sexual frenzy, grabbed the wall with the hand he'd been furiously pumping his dick with, speeded up dragging the musclegod's jock in his ass trench, and for the first time ever, shot a load without having his hand wrapped around his joystick. Danny held the jockstrap to his asscrack till his breathing returned to normal. He threw it in his gym bag and went home.

A few days later, Danny found himself working with Diesel at wrestling practice. The coach had randomly assigned partners (Diesel as co-captain was actually the one doing the pairings, though the team didn't know, and of course snatched Danny) and asked them to go through some light practice moves.

All Danny wanted to do was get through the moves without popping a boner. And he knew it was going to be very difficult. He'd beat off more times than he could count the last few days, thinking about

Diesel, smelling his jockstrap, sometimes even licking it, and most times, shooting in it.

Though the bright maroon and white school singlet Danny wore was a bit baggy (except around his butt of course), Diesel's was stretched over his muscled body in a way that left very little to the imagination.

"OK, Danny, let's try again," said Diesel as they circled each other, crouched, arms extended. Diesel was inches taller than Danny and close to a third over his weight — it was like a Hummer and a Mini Cooper facing off!

Danny lunged at Diesel, going under, reaching up and wrapping his arms around as much of Diesel's midsection as he could attempting to knock him off balance. All he managed to do was smash his head into the cleft between Diesel's hanging pecs. Diesel smiled as he landed a hand on each of Danny's butt cheeks, lifted him by them, flipped him in the air, and had Danny land on his back with a thump. Diesel stretched himself sideways across Danny's body, pinned him to the mat, and then purposely ground his hefty package into Danny's thigh.

"OK, OK, it was a stupid move. You can let me up," said Danny in a panic as he felt himself go instantly hard. It wasn't just the muscles, it was also the smell. Danny saw the jockstrap in his mind.

"Sorry, Danny, hope I didn't hurt you," said Diesel as he slid off Danny, stood up, and pulled Danny up. "Hey, what about you coming over to my place on Saturday? I've got a pretty nice gym area set up in my basement. We can work on some moves. Wadaya say, huh, squirt?" asked Diesel, again messing his short spiked blonde hair.

"That would be great, Diesel, just great. What time?" Danny could hardly believe this was happening.

"How 'bout noon? We can combine the workout with lunch. I make a mean peanut butter sandwich," said Diesel flashing a dazzling smile at Danny. "Just come on in, the door won't be locked. Just yell so I know you're there. OK, let's try something else, OK?" Diesel rubbed his shoulder straps in a distracted way, then reached down and adjusted his package. Danny couldn't help but stare at the sizable package.

They circled each other once again, eyes locked on each other. All Danny kept seeing were the muscles bulging and moving all over Diesel as he circled. All Diesel saw was a twink he had to have — soon. As Danny once again lunged at Diesel, he was surprised by Diesel's grabbing him at the waist, twisting and pulling Danny toward him as he fell backwards. Instinctively, Danny's arms grabbed, and ended up wrapped around one of Diesel's thighs. He was horrified as he realized that his face was smashed against Diesel's crotch. Diesel was on his back, legs spread, with Danny face down on top of him. He wrapped one arm near Danny's shoulders, pinning his upper body in place. His other paw landed smack on Danny's pert little ass, pressing it into his torso, while Danny's legs flopped uselessly off of Diesel's shoulder.

"This is a hold that a wrestler uses to intimidate and tire his opponent," Diesel explained to Danny, while gently and rhythmically pressing on Danny's ass. "Though you're on top, I'm able to keep my shoulders off the ground so the ref can't call in your favor. Your job is to flip me using your upper body strength, holding onto my legs, and flipping," said Diesel as he continued the rhythmic pressure on Danny's adorable bubblebutt.

Danny barely heard what Diesel was saying as his hard dick pressed into Diesel's chest and with each inhale of breath he took in the heady aroma of Diesel's crotch and then blew out hot air against Diesel's cock which seemed to be firming up and slowly expanding.

"Try, Danny, try!" ordered Diesel.

Danny let go of Diesel's thigh with one arm, wrapped it around Diesel's other thigh and pulled. He got nowhere. Diesel made sure to keep Danny's face pressed against his hardening trunk of a dick while relishing the feel of Danny's firm rounded ass.

"Ooh, yeah, this is one fine butt!" thought Diesel.

"Uugggghhhhh!" Danny's open mouth expelled onto Diesel's pulsing log as he shot a load of boycream into his jockstrap while pressed against Diesel's chest. Diesel smiled in triumph as he felt the vibrations from Danny's mouth on his cock and the throbbing dick on his chest.

"Took too long, Danny, let's try again," said Diesel as he let go of Danny. Danny fell off of Diesel, stayed in a crouched position for a moment, then said through uneven breaths, "I don't feel so good, Diesel, I gotta go," and lurched toward the locker room.

"I'll see you Saturday, Danny...remember, Noon, just come on in!" Diesel rubbed the wet spot under his hanging right pec and brought two fingers up to his mouth, relishing the taste of Danny's cum and remembering the feel of Danny's butt as it clenched in and out as he shot his load. Diesel flexed his prick, a burp of precum seeped out.

Danny had spent the whole morning Saturday agonizing over whether to go to Diesel's. He had avoided Diesel on campus the rest of the week, ashamed over what had happened at practice. In the end, he chose to head over to Diesel's place because he thought Diesel might get mad if he didn't show up, and because he could no longer deny his need to be near Diesel's hard body. The memory of Diesel's singlet covered prick pressed against his open mouth, slowly moving as if on its own power, wouldn't leave his head — he kept seeing a naked Diesel standing in front of him begging, "Suck me, Danny, make me cum, and let me fuck your sweet little ass!" Danny had been beating off regularly since then with that image in his head still using Diesel's now crusty jockstrap.

To add to his agony, he was now getting a twitching/itching feeling in his ass each time he got off. He had forced himself not to beat off for the last 24 hours, and it hadn't been easy. He finally got dressed — briefs, shorts, t-shirt and gym shoes. He threw his singlet and a clean jockstrap in a gym bag. At the last minute he pulled out Diesel's jockstrap, hidden in his underwear drawer, and slipped it into a side pocket of the bag.

"Diesel!" Danny yelled as he walked in the front door.

"I'll be right there, Danny. Meet me in the kitchen," Diesel called from upstairs. Danny made his way to the back of the house where he assumed the kitchen was. On the way, he stopped to admire some photos of Diesel on a hallway wall. There was Diesel as a cub scout, a boy scout, and lots of pictures with him holding different trophies, each accompanied with a big smile. Danny lingered over one where Diesel must have been about 12 or 13, just beginning to pack on some muscle. He was holding a trophy over his head with a swimmer balanced on top of it. Danny was transfixed with the size of the package Diesel had crammed inside his Speedos. It easily looked twice as big as what you'd expect on a kid that age and size. Danny made his way to the kitchen and sat at the table.

"Hey, guy, thanks for coming over. I missed seeing you around campus. Were you out sick?" asked Diesel as he walked into the kitchen clothed only in those same black nylon shorts and laced up boots. If anything, he looked even hotter than normal. He seemed to have veins popping out all over the place. The cords of muscle in his legs played tag with each other as he walked. His six pack bulged underneath the overhang of his pec slabs which rippled ever so slightly with each footfall. Truth was, Diesel has gone through a workout just before Danny got there so he'd be nice and pumped.

"Huh, you OK squirt?" asked Diesel as he moved up to Danny's seated form and rubbed the side of Danny's head, including an ear, rubbing more slowly than before, almost a caress.

"No, I'm fine. I was just pretty busy lately, lots of homework," replied Danny as he tried to stay focused, fighting the urges shooting through his body as Diesel rubbed his skull. And that damned tingling in his ass started.

"What's say we grab a bit of grub before working out? Not much, just enough to give us some energy so we both get a real workout. Sound good to you, bud?"

"Sure, Diesel, I'm a little hungry anyway," Danny lied. He was ready to do anything to avoid giving into the temptation of coming into contact with Diesel. He was starting to panic thinking that he'd been wrong to decide to come over.

"I make a mean peanut butter and honey sandwich. That OK with you?" Diesel moved behind the counter where the peanut butter, honey jar, and bread were already waiting. Danny's hungry eyes followed Diesel but had to eventually look away since the counter ledge was just about even with the waist of Diesel's low riding shorts. It was too easy for Danny to imagine that Diesel was actually naked on the other side of the counter. Danny's mind imagined hearing Diesel's cock bouncing against the cabinet drawer fronts under the counter.

Diesel set a sandwich down in front of Danny, pulled up a chair next to him and sat facing Danny, legs spread. He waited while Danny started eating his sandwich. He eyed Danny's small frame, imagining rubbing his hands all over it.

"So, do I win the blue ribbon?"

"It's real good, Diesel, real good. I never had honey with peanut butter before. I really like it," said Danny, meaning it.

Diesel smiled and picked up his sandwich, taking a big bite, chewing slowly as he held the sandwich inches from his mouth, eyeing Danny hungrily. He took another bite. Honey oozed out of the bottom of the sandwich and dripped in heavy plops near the top of Diesel's left pec. Danny stared straight ahead. Diesel squeezed his sandwich; more honey landed on his pec and began slowly moving southward.

"Oh, shit!"

Danny jerked his head sideways to see what the matter was.

"Fuck, I am such a slob," Diesel laughed as he leaned toward Danny, touching one of the lines of thick honey making their way down his chest, spreading his legs even more. "Uummm," said Diesel as he slowly licked the finger he had caught some of the loose honey on, "tastes real good." Danny had stopped chewing and just stared at Diesel's finger as it moved from pec to lips, and then Diesel's mouth sucking on the finger.

"Try some, squirt, it's better warmed up," said Diesel as he moved a finger toward Danny's open mouth. Danny was frozen. Diesel's finger slid into Danny's mouth and made slow circles on his tongue. Danny instinctively closed his lips around the fat moving digit. As Diesel slowly pulled his finger out of Danny's mouth, he put his other hand at the back of Danny's head.

"Here, Danny, its better from the source," he whispered as he drew Danny's head toward his now heaving pec. Danny's mind went blank as his mouth opened and suctioned onto Diesel's sticky chest.

"Oh...baby...that feels so good. I've been dreaming about something like this since we worked out together the other day, Danny. You are the cutest little fucker...and that ass of yours...made in heaven." Diesel guided Danny's mouth around his chest. Danny sucked on the smooth flesh, quickly taking in all the honey. Diesel pulled Danny's head off his chest.

"Danny, I really really like you and want to make you feel good. Will you let me do that?" Diesel stared into Danny's wide unfocused beautiful brown eyes. He took Danny's t-shirt off over his head and began rubbing Danny's smooth stomach, feeling the tight small six pack, and gently pinching the already erect nipples. Diesel threw Danny over his shoulder, grabbed the jar of honey and Danny's gym bag, and headed for the basement.

Diesel did have a pretty well equipped gym in his basement. There were different kinds of equipment all over the place. At one end, blue mats covered the floor facing a wall of mirrors. Diesel used this area for his before and after workout stretching exercises, and to practice poses. He sat Danny on the mats leaning him against a weight bench.

"You are the most beautiful guy I've ever seen, Danny, did you know that?" said Diesel as he first removed Danny's shoes and then began lightly rubbing Danny's extended legs. Danny stared at Diesel and slowly spread his legs wider, thinking that he might be dreaming.

Tears filled Danny's eyes. "Diesel, you are the most beautiful guy I've ever seen. I know it's not right for me to feel this way about you, but I can't help it."

"What do you mean 'not right', Danny? There's nothing wrong with a guy thinking another guy is great looking. Hell, half the reason I've got the body I have is so other guys will appreciate it." Diesel stood up, never losing eye contact with Danny, and slowly pulled off his black shorts, and then the flimsy jockstrap that was doing a very poor job of holding his prick and balls in one place.

"You like?" he asked as he hit a double bicep pose. Danny stood up, mesmerized by the sight in front of him, and yanked off the rest of his own clothing. The two guys stood facing each other; both looked sideways in the mirrors Diesel's huge form towered over Danny's, whose slim cock was rock hard, pointing upward like a compass dial toward Diesel's marbled cocked and enormous churning balls. They looked back at each other, eyes filled with the need to rut.

"Go ahead, Danny, tell me, show me .."

Danny reached out, placing both hands on Diesel's six pack. They stood still. Diesel was ready to give the kid anything he wanted, because he knew the prize waiting for him — Danny's ass was going to be his. Danny pressed on the lumpy flesh of Diesel's abs, awed at the feel of the firmness. Diesel felt the heat of Danny's palms and fingers, and put a hand on either side of Danny's head, cocked it upward so their eyes met, "Tell me what you want, little guy. What will make you feel good?" The basement was hotter than the rest of the house. That and the passion in the air had both males covered with sweat.

"Turn around...please," Danny croaked. Diesel complied. Danny was suddenly a bit light headed staring at the hard round slabs of ass in front of him. He put both hands on the left cheek, and let out a soft moan as he reacted to the heat of Diesel's flesh, and the way the cheek changed shape as Diesel tensed it in reaction to the touch. Danny moved his right hand to the right ass cheek, moving forward as he began squeezing them.

"Lay down."

Diesel got on his stomach, extending his arms and legs outward, tensed in a full body stretch. Danny stared at the male mass at his feet, hoping he'd always remember the sight. He took note of Diesel's body hair. He'd always liked the way Diesel's curly blonde hair fell in his eyes, but he'd never taken the time to note the downy light hairs covering Diesel's legs. But what surprised him was the tuft of darker blonde hair at the base of Diesel's spine draining into his asscrack. Danny picked up the bottle of honey, straddled Diesel's prone body, and sat on his back facing Diesel's ass and spread legs. Slowly tipping the bottle, he watched the honey fall and land on the inner ridge of one of Diesel's cheeks, and moved the bottle slightly so it crossed the crack and hit the other cheek before setting the bottle down.

Danny rubbed the honey into Diesel's skin. His mouth went slack as he watched the muscles in Diesel's ass cheeks ripple as Diesel tensed and released them over and over, pressing his dick into the mat. Danny covered the patch of hair near the asscrack with his honey coated hands playing with pushing the hair in different directions. By now Diesel's breath was ragged.

"Oh, Danny, fuuuucckkkk...that feels so gooooood..."

Danny laid down on Diesel's large back, each foot pressing against one of Diesel's outstretched biceps, his mouth hovering near Diesel's ass, hands curving around Diesel's waist, resting on the mats. Drool fell from Danny's mouth, landing on the honey coated tuft. Danny moved his open mouth to retrieve the spit and was rewarded with the sweet taste of honey. He swirled the hair with his tongue and then planted his open mouth on the spot, his nose resting at the beginning of Diesel's asscrack, his forehead pressed against the flexing ass cheeks. As his mouth slowly moved further along the great divide, Danny started flexing his own ass as he pressed his throbbing dick against Diesel's muscled back. Diesel's head was turned toward the mirror and he groaned as he watched the twink's body resting on his ocean of a body, with Danny's ass gently bobbing up and down. "Fuck, I can hardly wait to take this kid!" thought Diesel.

Danny pulled Diesel's ass cheeks apart as he dove for more of the honey, and discovered to his frenzied delight, more hair in the trench. His thrusts on Diesel's back quickened. His climax caught him by surprise as his focus had been on lapping up the prized liquid. He felt at least five good pumps of his juice spread out between his stomach and Diesel's back flesh, all the while grunting into Diesel's ass. With one of the pumps, his mouth opened and then lightly bit the flesh of Diesel's ass. Diesel let out a squeak as his body jerked slightly in reaction.

The two wrestlers stayed like this for a few minutes, taking deep breaths in unison. Danny finally sat up. Joining the noise of their breathing was the sucking sound of the seal of Danny's cum being broken between their bodies. Diesel turned over on his back, sending Danny sideways to the floor. Diesel quickly picked up Danny by his tiny waist and placed him on his stomach. They stared at each other hungrily. Diesel's eyes were hot with desire; Danny's lids rested half closed as he basked in his post climactic haze.

"How ya feelin', Danny? Feelin' good? I am. You made my ass feel so good with your tongue. You're very talented, and very cute." Diesel ran his hands over Danny's torso and up and down his arms. Danny just sat there, relaxed and satiated then he fell forward, his mouth landed on the side of Diesel's neck. He cock, still hard, slid in the crevices of Diesel's abs. While Danny sucked on Diesel's neck, Diesel started rubbing Danny's back, up and down. Eventually his paws moved to that prized mound, Danny's ass.

"You want me to make you feel even better, Danny? And it would make me feel great too. Wadaya say, squirt?"

Danny pushed himself up from Diesel's body, "What do you mean?"

Diesel kept rubbing Danny's ass and his legs. "I gotta get my nut off, and it has to be up that tight little ass!" thought Diesel. "I mean, can I fuck you, little guy? Can I put my dick in your ass? It's gonna make you feel better than you've ever felt in your life, I swear," Diesel pulled Danny's face to his and they moaned sucking on each other's open mouths.

Danny pulled away, a line of spit curving outward between their mouths. "That thing would never fit! Are you nuts or are you just kidding?" asked Danny, nervously, with a smile.

Diesel pretended that he was hurt. "I'm sorry, Danny, it's just that I thought you liked me and wanted to make me feel as good as I made you feel." By now he had grabbed Danny's waist and was sliding Danny's body up and down his own. "If you don't trust me, well..."

"Of course I trust you, Diesel! You've been nicer to me than just about anyone ever. If you think you can fit your dick in me, I trust you."

"Oh, Danny, you are too much!" Diesel pulled him down in another long sucking kiss. "C'mere," said Diesel as he dragged himself toward the wall, ending up leaning on an angled piece of covered foam. Diesel wanted to be able to see the show. He wanted to be propped up as the kid got spiked on his post. Danny walked over. Diesel handed him some Astroglide.

"Rub this stuff on my dick. It will make it real slick." Diesel had to work to control his building sexual frenzy. What he really wanted to do was slam the kid up against the wall and hammer him with his dick till he got off. But he knew if he was patient, he'd end up with a better reward.

Danny squeezed a few drops of the clear liquid on Diesel's cock. Diesel was in a semi-seated position and his massive vein covered dick was still pointing southward. Danny also squeezed a couple of drops on his hands. He figured that sitting on Diesel facing his dick was the best angle. Diesel's breath started coming a little more quickly as he stared at Danny's back, realizing that the kid was really focusing on lubing his horse cock.

Diesel lifted Danny and turned him around so they faced each other. "I gotta get you ready too, Danny. Give me the lube." Diesel squeezed some lube on his hands and reached under Danny with one hand, working it up and down Danny's crack, frequently playing with Danny's puckered asshole with one of his fingers. Danny had meanwhile fallen forward and his hands were on Diesel's shoulders.

"Danny, do me a favor? Would you play with my tits? Please? It will make me feel really good." Danny's eyes popped open. He couldn't believe Diesel was asking, almost begging him to do that. Danny loved Diesel's chest. He put a hand on each mound of flesh and began squeezing.

"Oh, God, Danny, yes, that's it. Squeeze them...pull 'em...hit 'em if you want to."

A yelp of surprise came out of Danny as Diesel's finger poked inside his asshole. "It's OK, buddy, trust me. I'm just makin' sure that you're ready. In a minute, you're gonna feel really really nice," said Diesel as he slipped in a second finger. Danny focused on how good Diesel's pecs felt. Every once in a while, Diesel would flex them, making Danny chuckle a bit, and then Danny would pound the flesh harder.

"Go ahead, it's OK," said Diesel as he sensed from the look in Danny's eyes that he wanted to have his mouth on the pecs. Diesel was used to guys being fascinated by his mammoth slabs of muscle there. Besides, he wanted something to keep the kid distracted.

As Danny's mouth suctioned on Diesel's right tit, Diesel jammed a third finger into the tight little bubblebutt. Danny groaned on the tit. Diesel began pumping his fingers in and out of the tight chute. With his other hand, he gently caressed Danny's head.

"I think we're ready, Danny," said Diesel working really hard to control his lust. He pulled his fingers slowly out of Danny's ass, longing to keep them in there. But he thought about how good his dick was going to feel jammed into that tight space.

Danny lifted his head up, his mouth stayed slack, a bit of spit ran down to his chin. Sitting up again, he felt Diesel's monster pressing against his back.

"What do I do, Diesel?"

"You're going to be the one in charge here, Danny. You decide how much is going in. Here, let me put a bit more on," Danny stood up, straddling Diesel, as Diesel grabbed the lube. Danny's eyes glazed over as he bent over and watched Diesel squeezed a few more drops of lube onto his already shiny dick and rub it all over. It reminded Danny of the honey; he imagined sucking honey off that dick.

"OK, big guy, just sit down on it."

Danny sat down on what felt like a tree trunk. Diesel's heat seeking dickhead was at its target. "It will help if you pretend you have to take a shit. Your muscles will relax. Trust me, Danny, do it."

And Danny did. But little progress was made.

"It's not goin' anywhere, Diesel," Danny whined.

"Try harder, Danny. It's the only way. Try really hard."

Diesel had his legs drawn up so that Danny could rest his hands on Diesel's knees, Danny leaned his torso back. Diesel's slick lube covered hands kept up a constant rubbing on either of Danny's sides, from his ankles up to his armpits.

"Look at me, Danny. Focus on my eyes. You can do this if you want, Danny. Do it." Danny sat up and saw love and lust in Diesel's eyes, and he wanted to please Diesel. He grunted and pushed. "That's it, buddy, you can do it!" Danny's head jerked up and his mouth opened wide as his asshole opened and Diesel's huge dickhead eased in.

"That's it, Danny, you did it! The rest is gonna be easy," lied Diesel. It had been a while since Diesel's dick was this hard. He was surprised at how turned on his was by this guy wanting to make him feel good. Danny groaned his way down a few more inches.

"That's it, Diesel, I can't do any more. It hurts when I push."

"We just need more lube, babe, that's all. Pull up and I'll take care of it. Danny's legs quivered as he attempted to stand.

"I'm stuck, Diesel, help me!" Danny panicked. Diesel knew that Danny's ass had just tried to clamp shut during the exit. Of course, he also knew that his large dickhead would not make for an exit easy.

"It's OK, buddy, you don't need to go all the way." Diesel quickly globed on more lube. Holding Danny's waist with one hand, he ran the other one up and down his dick, rubbing a finger up Danny's trench on each trip upwards.

"OK, try again, Danny...and relax...you're gonna feel so good...real soon."

Danny's hands each grabbed a knee of Diesel's and he focused on pushing down. It not only felt really weird to be putting something in a place where before today only things came out of, but it also hurt...a lot more than he was letting Diesel know. His eyes roamed over the propped body in front of him. He was really turned on knowing how turned on Diesel was. Diesel kept rubbing Danny's body, while his own sweat covered body heaved in and out with deep breaths.

"Ooowwwww!" yelled Danny, "It hurts Diesel, really bad." Tears started mixing with the sweat on his face.

Diesel wasn't about to stop. In desperation, he reached over to Danny's gym bag, groping. He grabbed some material and pulled. It was a jockstrap, and from the looks of it, pretty dirty. As Diesel pulled the jock closer to both of them, he saw the faded magic marker "D" on it, identifying it as his.

"You little sneak, you!" said Diesel, holding the stiff dirty jock in front of Danny's now shocked face. "You stole my jockstrap. How long have you had this?" Diesel knew exactly where the kid got it. He had lots of jocks, and he used them as bait all the time. It sure looked to Diesel like this kid had added quite a few loads of cum to the mix.

"I'm sorry, Diesel. You left it in the locker room. I was going to clean it for you and give it back. I swear!"

"Don't cry about it, squirt. It's OK. I know why you took it...and I'm flattered." Diesel brought the jock to his nose and sniffed. "Ah, smells like there's more here than my sweat."

"I...I...I...," stammered Danny.

Diesel caressed Danny's face with his free hand. "Don't say anything, Danny. I'm honored...really." He then brought the jock to the other side of Danny's face and began rubbing the rough material on his cheek and then back into Danny's sweaty scalp and neck. The material began softening as it soaked in the sweat.

"I was just trying to find something to help you, and I think this is the best thing for that. You ever see those movies where they get the guy to bite down on something while they remove a bullet or something?" Danny nodded slowly. "Well, if you bite down on this," said Diesel as he dragged the jockstrap across Danny's mouth, "it should help. C'mon...open...bite."

Danny opened, Diesel pushed. Stifling a gag, Danny bit down. Diesel's hands roamed over Danny's chest, pinching his nipples, and then rested on the kid's waist. Danny bit harder and pushed. Though he didn't know, he now had half of Diesel's log inside him. Diesel grabbed Danny's waist harder in his excitement.

"That's it, Danny, you're doin' a fuckin' great job! Stop pushing for a sec...just rest." Diesel wanted to savor what he was feeling right now. He looked at his mammoth dick with Danny perched on it, and then looked up to Danny's face. Danny had a pleading look in his eyes. His teeth gripped the soggy jockstrap, a bit of spittle ran out of one corner of his mouth. Diesel flexed his cock. Danny jerked, lifted his head, and let out a muffled moan without releasing the jockstrap.

"Yeah...told you you were gonna feel good. That's a little joy buzzer you got in your butt that only my dick can ring. Wanna feel that again?" Danny nodded slowly. Diesel gave his dick a pump. Danny's head fell back as a quieter but longer moan escaped.

"It's gonna get even better now, Danny. Sit down some more. Come all the way home, little buddy," said Diesel as his hands holding Danny's waist pulled down a bit. Danny yelped. Diesel stopped pulling and began pushing Danny up...an inch...another inch...then he pulled down, harder than before, stopping only when Danny's insides refused to make any more room. Diesel repeated his move.

"OK, now you do it by yourself, Danny." Danny moved his hands from Diesel's knees to midway on this thighs, and began fucking himself with Diesel's pole. Each time he bottomed out, he hit that buzzer Diesel told him about; and each time he felt an electrical jolt travel all through his body and end at his throbbing penis. He noticed that a thick stream of precum now connected his hard dick to Diesel's stomach. He watched the muscles in Diesel's arms ripple as he held Danny at the waist. He paid no attention to the fact that Diesel was gradually taking over the driver's seat in their fucking.

Diesel was losing control. He'd never had his dick in anything this tight and this hot. It was so hot and yet it didn't burn. It was so tight and yet it didn't hurt. It reminded him of the time he tricked with this biker guy who beat Diesel off while wearing leather gloves. The guy had huge hands. When he wrapped the thin fitted leather gloves around Diesel's hard-on, he kept up a steady and really firm pressure as he slid up and down with a bit of a swirling motion. Diesel remembered that it felt like his dick was inside something really tight and warm, yet he could see it being jacked off in front of him. He also remembered that it was a great climax...all over the guy's face.

Back to now. Diesel easily lifted Danny up and down on his dick which now started to hurt with the need to shoot. Diesel quickened the pace, starting to really pull hard on the downward thrusts, grunting with the effort to get his entire member in that hot tunnel. His hands almost touched reaching around the kid's slim waist. Danny entered some other kind of dimension as he was quickly overloaded with the combination of ecstasy and pain he was feeling. Diesel stared at his dick, watching a bit more of it disappear into Danny's steaming insides with each downward pull. He was sweating so much, he had to blink his eyes a lot to keep the sweat from blurring his vision. His hands started slipping on Danny's wet body. Diesel squeezed tighter. Danny was now a rag doll. His arms and legs seemed to be filled with jelly rather than bone and muscle.

Diesel felt his cum rounding to the home stretch. He was taking short speedy intakes of breath, working not to pass out in ecstasy. Suddenly, he was there. He jammed Danny onto his dick one last time, pulled Danny's torso to him slamming his forehead into Danny's chest and released shot after shot after shot of his cumsnot inside Danny. He could feel it shooting out and the gradually forming a liquid barrier around his shaft between it and Danny's insides.

Diesel heaved out load after load of air from his lungs, spit shooting out of his mouth along with the air. Ever so slowly, he came down from the high. Finally, he pulled his head away from Danny and pushed Danny back a bit so he was sitting straight up on Diesel's dick. The first thing he noticed was that Danny's ass rested on Diesel's pubic hair — score! He got it all in. The second thing he noticed was a drop of cum on his lower lip — a glance to Danny's crotch confirmed that the kid had shot off once again. The third thing he noticed was that his old jockstrap was hanging out of Danny's mouth, hooked to one of his teeth by a thin piece of elastic thread — it looked completely soaked. The fourth thing he noticed was that Danny was either dead or passed out.

He pulled the jockstrap off, tossed t aside, grabbed Danny's chin and shook it violently and then started slapping him, "Hey, Danny, wake up...where are ya, buddy?" Danny's eyes opened slightly, his breathing was shallow.

"God, Diesel,..." Danny's arms rested at his side. Diesel massaged Danny's stomach. Danny tightened his ass muscles; Diesel flexed his dick in response, and was shocked to realize he felt Danny's stomach bulge ever so slightly. Thinking it was just Danny breathing; he tried flexing his cock again, and again felt the bulge. Removing his hand, he stared disbelievingly at Danny's stomach. Through the trails of sweat running down, he saw the outline of Danny's small tight six pack, and flexed his tool ceep inside. Danny's stomach bulged forward a bit — Diesel found it sexy as hell. Diesel took Danny's left hand and put it on his stomach.

"Feel this," said Diesel as he locked eyes with Danny and pulsed. Danny's eyes got big as he realized what he was feeling. Danny fell forward and locked his mouth onto Diesel's.

"I don't think I can stand up, Diesel, my legs are numb or something," breathed Danny into Diesel's face after the kiss. "I think I need your help." Danny leaned up.

Diesel had slid down some on the foam pad he'd been propped against. He now scooted down so he was flat on the mat, but kept his legs bent for Danny to lean back on. He grabbed Danny's waist and pushed up. Danny moaned as he was lifted off the spike. His insides started doing all kinds of summersaults as the invading log retreated.

Diesel stared at his dick, shocked at its size in comparison to what it was exiting. Danny involuntarily squeezed his ass muscles, loose as they were, and "caught" himself on the ridge of Diesel's dickhead. Diesel gritted his teeth and pushed harder, lifting Danny up and forward a bit, freeing him with a small suctioning noise.

Cum, lube and Danny's own fluids began running down his legs and onto the sides of Diesel's torso where Danny's feet dangled. Danny let out a loud watery fart, giggled, and some heavy streams of the liquid mixture fell directly onto Diesel's chest. Diesel gently lowered Danny to a kiss, their bodies pressed together, sealed by their own juices. Diesel put his hands on Danny's ass grabbing a cheek in each hand, the ass he now owned, and began sliding Danny's body onto his.

"My butt feels funny and sore!" said Danny propping himself on his elbows, pressing them into Diesel's relaxed pec flesh.

"You'll be sore for a bit but you'll get back to normal in no time. Trust me, OK?"

"Hey, can I try something?" Danny asked hesitantly.

Diesel was a bit surprised, "What?"

Danny slid around so that they were in a 69 position and put both his hands on Diesel's fat cock as it rested on Diesel's stomach. He squeezed with both hands and discovered that it was pretty firm, even when it wasn't hard as steel and shooting buckets of cum.

"What are you doing, Danny?" Diesel, still in the relaxed after sex mode, stretched his whole body with a big yawn. "Fuck, I've still got my boots on!" The small warm hands ministering to his dick felt really nice. He was getting hard again. Then he felt something wet and cool hit his cockskin. Danny had picked up the jar of honey and was pouring some on Diesel as he kept squeezing and rubbing with his other hand. He set the jar down and started rubbing the honey all over Diesel's cock and balls. It mixed with the leftover scum from the wild fuck, but Diesel's nostrils were filled with the odor of honey.

"Uuuuugggggghhhhhh," came out of Diesel's mouth as he felt Danny's lips kissing near his piss slit. He put his hands on Danny's butt, staring at the almost inhumanly stretched hole. Diesel began squeezing Danny's buttcheeks.

"Oh, God, Diesel, you have the biggest dick in the world! Can I have it all to myself forever?" he asked with a grin stretching around to look at Diesel.

"Hey, it's yours right now, little guy. Take it to town."

Danny returned to the throbbing love muscle. He started sucking it all over, almost chewing on it to get at the honey. He then went back to the tip, opened his mouth wide, and attempted to swallow it hole. All he managed was the head, his lips sealing like a clamp around the ridge of the dickhead. He loved the way he could feel Diesel's veins as they shifted under his moving hands.

"Oh, little buddy, you are the best..." sighed Diesel as he got hotter. He couldn't help but join in by thrusting his cock inside Danny's tiny grip. "Uuggg...uuugggghhhh...here it comes!" Diesel yelled as he tensed his whole body, squeezing Danny's asscheeks together.

Danny was determined to suck up every last drop but wasn't prepared for the volume of Diesel's load. The first shot went straight to the back of his throat. While attempting to swallow it, a second shot, equally large, pumped out. Danny popped off the head and pulled away, choking, holding the firehose as it sprayed all over him.

As Danny recovered from his face wash, Diesel realized that at least one shot of his cum must have grazed over Danny's blonde hair as he licked some warm splooge off the back of one of his hands.

"Let's say you and me take a shower, huh squirt?" said Diesel as he gently eased himself out from under Danny's cum and sweat soaked body.

"I don't think I can stand, Diesel. My butt really hurts and my legs are shaking," said Danny looking up at his musclegod who seemed to shine with the mix of fluids coating him. Though tired and hurting, Danny kept his hard-on drinking in the sight of Diesel towering over him.

"Hey, I need your help getting all this clean; you need to scrub these real good," Diesel flashed his biggest smile at the younger wrestler laying at his feet as he put one hand behind his now resting dick and balls, pushing them forward toward Danny. He stooped, picked Danny up in his arms, and headed for the shower.

"Let's you and me clean each other off real good, order a pizza, watch a movie, and then we'll discuss dessert." Danny rested his head against Diesel's chest and started sucking one of Diesel's nipples and playing with the other.

CHAPTER 4

The Photo Sessions

"Louder!" yelled Diesel. Rob cranked the CD as high as he could stand it. The throbbing house music was about to start affecting his shooting ability. He pulled the camera from his eye for a moment, looked directly at Diesel gyrating in that skin-tight singlet, and decided it was worth it. The moment he set eyes on this guy, he knew he had a winner.

Lots of guys responded to the ads Rob had posted around town promising quick good money for some male modeling. Most knew exactly what was up when they called. Rob would meet them, talk, take a Polaroid or two, and give the old, "I'll get back to you." Most, he never did.

Diesel was memorable from the start...showed up for the interview wearing a pink wife beater that stopped above his naval, low rider black Levis that barely contained his ass, sandals, mirrored sunglasses that he seemed very attached to, and the final touch, a pair of leather police search gloves. Rob couldn't tell which feature of this blonde muscletoy was his best: ass, crotch, chest, abs, legs, arms, face...he was all that and more. Rob was interested.

"None," he said in answer to Rob's questions about having any inhibitions. He was cockier than most guys Rob met, and seemed to have the packaging to support it. Background included lots of sports, and he claimed he did yoga for relaxation. He had a nice even tan and from the surface area showing, great skin — both meant minimal body make-up needs, a real plus.

Rob was happy to hear him say he was 23 and a senior in college. He actually carried a copy of his birth certificate to prove it. He said though he knows he looks of age to most people, some guys are jealous enough to give him a hard time so the birth certificate shuts them up. Rob didn't really care. He just needed the right packaging. And every part of Diesel was giving the right answer.

Rob explained about needing to take some Polaroid's. His plan was to take full body shots from different angles. Though he never asked the men at this point to remove any clothing, he did not discourage it if they wanted to.

"Do I need to pose or something?"

"Why, have you modeled before?"

"Shit, no! But I was thinking it might be more fun if I just kind of moved around and you took pictures. Isn't that how they do it? Can we do that?"

This was a first. "Sure, would it help if I put on some music?"

"Naw, don't bother." And he started to move. Maybe 'move' isn't the right word for what Diesel did. He started a swaying motion that suddenly seemed to have many parts of his body moving in sensual rolls — Rob quickly grabbed his camera. After a few minutes, Diesel grabbed the bottom of his wife beater, "OK?" he asked Rob, motioning that he wanted to take it off.

"Fine, Diesel, keep going."

Diesel pulled it off and revealed his amazing chest — two great slabs of pectoral muscle, hanging like snow ready to avalanche over his sculpted abs. He turned in a circle, rotating his hips lewdly the whole way. Next he kicked off the sardals. Diesel faced away from the camera and undid his low r ders. Arms then shot up in the air as he danced to a tune in his head. The pants started slipping but his bubble butt kept the pants from going further. Then he faced the camera. The only place his hair darkened at all was his treasure trail — and it was thicker than you'd think on a younger blonde guy. Diesel pulled his pants off.

What remained was nothing short of a wet dream. Rob took quite a few more Polaroid's than he usually did. The sight of this tanned bunch of muscle, covered only by an old jock, sunglasses and the leather gloves was about more than Rob could handle...and this was supposed to be an initial interview! Diesel kept running his hands over his body, almost as if he couldn't believe how fine it actually was.

"Whoa, cowboy, I've seen enough!"

Diesel stopped suddenly and stood there panting, looking at the photographer. Those pouty open lips quivered slightly as the heavy breathing went in and out.

"What's wrong? There something you don't like?" Diesel pushed the glasses on top of his head into his blonde curls, his warm blue eyes only added to the package.

"Quite the contrary. I like all that I see," Rob said as he gave Diesel a blatant elevator look. Diesel seemed quite happy with the response as a smile broke out on his face. "Can you come next week? You'd be modeling athletic wear and such. Pay is $50 an hour, cash. There could be bonuses too. Interested?"

"Sure, I'm interested. I can come whenever you want me to... whenever and wherever," smirked Diesel as he adjusted his sizable dick in the worn jock.

"The kid's comin' on to me," thought Rob. "I smell a mother lode here...built like a brick shithouse...and cocky, real cocky...maybe Casey...," Rob's thought trailed off as he realized Diesel was just standing there.

"Next Tuesday, 7PM...that work for you?"

"Seven is great. I finish wrestling practice by 6:30, that gives me time to swing home, change and get over here on my bike." Diesel turned to get his clothes behind him. He bent over and Rob couldn't help but notice that the bubble butt was as equally muscular as it was prominent. "I bet that kid could cut off the blood supply of any dick, if the dick could first force its way in," thought Rob.

That was three weeks ago. Diesel was now back for his third modeling session. The first had been mainly different jeans and shorts topped with muscle t's — nothing too racy, but stretched out over Diesel's body and under the skilled shutters of Rob, the photos certainly were. The second session moved on to mainly swimwear and underwear. Diesel seemed to be relaxing into the work. This second time he asked for some music. Unbelievably, it seemed to inspire him to move in even more outrageous ways.

At the end of the second session, as he was counting out the 10's and 20's into Diesel's hand, Rob asked him if he'd consider coming straight to the next session from wrestling practice so he could shoot him in his singlet.

"Sure, that'd be great! I smell a bit ripe after practice, so I'll shower first, and then head over."

"Don't worry about it, Diesel. I want to capture what a real wrestler looks like and the smell will probably help both of us."

Diesel chuckled. He had no reservations now about being naked in front of Rob. During their conversation, Diesel took his time getting back into the running shorts and old t-shirt he arrived in. Rob noted that Diesel wasn't wearing underwear that day. Though he'd taken many shots of Diesel's crotch, this was the first time he was seeing the prize unwrapped. He couldn't help but notice the size of Diesel's dick. It looked like it was about as wide as it was long...and it was long.

"That reminds me, Rob — can I suggest something? I am actually having fun doing these shoots. I don t know what you do with these photos and I don't really care. But you mentioned the first time the possibility of bonuses and I thought of something. What would you say if during a shoot, if I asked, "More?", meaning somehow going further with whatever I'm doing, and you agree, it's an automatic extra $10 an hour?"

"You sneaky little businessman, you! OK. It's a deal."

"Thanks, Rob, you won't regret this. And that's $10 EACH time, right?"

"Each time, musclehead. Now get outta here."

The next week, Diesel decided to take his teasing of Rob to the next level. He loved the fact that he was getting paid cash to show off his body. Rob really had no idea how much Diesel enjoyed the photo sessions. When he finished practice, he took off his singlet and jockstrap, and changed into the singlet he had worn when he wrestled in high school. At the time, he was so looking forward to wrestling in high school, that he wore the singlet every chance he got. It was already too small for him by the end of his freshman year of high school and he got another one, but kept that first one.

Now he slipped into it, without his jock, and surveyed the results in the locker room mirror. "Shit! I'd fuck you if I could!" he whispered to his reflection. Diesel had long ago decided that it must have been a gay guy who came up with the design for his high school singlet — the blue and yellow were still quite bright, though through age and the extra stretching that his now larger body gave the material, it was a lot easier to see his body's definition. The electric blue singlet had two yellow stripes coming down each side to the waist where they then curved forward meeting at the crotch. Anyone looking at the singlet couldn't help by have their eyes get directed straight between the wrestler's thighs. And of course the rear had the yellow stripes directing your vision to the ass.

Diesel reached in and pointed his still flaccid joint sideways so it wouldn't be uncomfortable while on the bike. He put on a pair of shorts, threw the rest of his stuff in his gym bag, and headed outside to his bike to get to Rob's. He knew that this was the time to try out the new bonus program, hoping that Rob wouldn't be able to say No.

So there they were, in Rob's studio with Diesel grinding away to the pounding house music in that impossibly skin tight singlet that had everything except a big neon sign saying: Musclehead With Huge Dick — Come 'n Get It!

Rob went back to taking shots. Diesel peeled his right shoulder straps off. His right pec started bouncing more freely. The nipple was still covered, barely.

"More?"

Rob took the camera from his eye and nodded. Diesel pulled the other strap off and remained facing Rob but still rocking his body. With his shoulders bared, they suddenly looked even wider than they had a minute ago. Rob knew it was just a matter of perception, but he didn't care, he just wanted to get it on film. Diesel started rotating his shoulders in addition to the other movement. This allowed his chest to suddenly pop free of the tight clinging singlet as it rolled down and caught itself under the overhang of Diesel's pecs. Rob had been getting aroused, but at this sight, he went immediately to wood. Diesel danced to the throbbing music for almost ten minutes like that. His pecs were big enough that sometimes, when they weren't tensed, they went one way, while he went another.

"More?"

"Yes!"

Diesel pulled the singlet down a few inches below his belly button. His crotch now had a second layer of material covering it, and bulged out even more obscenely. Diesel went back to moving more freely, turning, twisting, bending, and moving around the room. Rob followed like a male dog scenting a bitch in heat. This went on for another ten minutes.

"That's it, captain...I'm beat...gotta take a break," said Diesel as he plopped down on a stool, panting. Large beads of sweat dotted his skin. He leaned forward, hands on his knees, trying to get his breath under control, pecs hanging deliciously. Rob kept clicking and clicking.

"Interested in making some extra money doing a special shoot?"

"How much, and what kind of special shoot?" asked Diesel sitting upright, legs spread, sweat pouring all over him.

"A friend of mine, Casey, likes to have photos of himself with younger guys — hot lookin' guys who show appreciation for his body. He's asked me to let him know whenever I find a guy who might work out well doing it."

"That's fag stuff," said Diesel as he stood up, pulled up one strap of the singlet and walked toward his gym bag.

"Doesn't mean it's *your* fag stuff. Look, he gets off on having a really hot guy 'pretend' to find him really hot. He just likes guys to touch him and tell him how hot he is. He's into leather. All you'd have to do is make a fuss over him. Sometimes there's some kissing involved. If things get really hot, you might end up beating each other off. That would be the limit. And the kissing and beating off hardly ever happens. Pay is $500, cash."

"$500? That's a nice chunk o' change. I don't know though, all that gay stuff. And what do you mean by `he's into leather'?"

"He likes to wear leather. And he likes the other guy to do the same. I show him a few of the pictures I take and he decides what he'd like you to wear. Diesel, trust me, I know he'd be really hot for you — you're his type — and you're a very talented model. I can tell that you're really proud of your body, and with good reason. Do this for the money and let the old guy get his jollies," Rob said casually, hoping to get Diesel interested. "He likes to set up a story for him and the other guy to follow. You should think of it like you're playing a character in a movie. It could be a lot of fun."

Diesel stood there contemplating the offer.   Truth was he had no trouble with doing anything with another guy — he actually preferred guys. Guys knew how to appreciate his body. He figured that whatever this older guy's scene was, he could end up making it about himself and not the other guy. Diesel thought that it might be fun to pretend to find another guy really hot. His dick started thickening.

"How `bout $700, Diesel? And if it gets to the beating off stage, I'll make it $1000," said Rob, drinking in the sight of the pumped up wrestler's body, head hanging with those blonde waves reaching downward, one hand on his chin, the other rubbing a hip. The yellow arrow on the singlet drawing Rob's eyes to the monster at its tip.

"OK, but if things get weird, I get to stop it at any point. Deal?"

"Deal. Now, can I take some shots of you in a bit of leather? You know, for Casey to look at? It won't take long."

"Sure, but the only leather thing I've got are my gloves."

"No prob, big guy. I keep some leather and other stuff in the wardrobe with the mirrored doors in the changing room. Why don't you pick some stuff out. Surprise me," Rob chuckled.

Diesel went beyond 'surprise'. "How's this?" Diesel stepped into the studio — leather shorts, an arm band around each bicep, big ass boots coming half way up his calves, a tight pullover armless top that made it down to the top of his abs, gloves — all black — and mirrored sunglasses. For a guy who didn't own much leather, he sure had a sense for what would make him stand out.

"I think I'll need the music. This leather feels kinda funny, but good," said Diesel as he admired himself in one of the mirrors.

Rob started the same CD and Diesel started to move — Rob started to shoot. Rob noticed that Diesel seemed to be touching and rubbing himself more than usual. "Must be the leather," thought Rob. Diesel put his hands on his ass, gyrating, making it look like he was guiding its direction with his hands. His gloved hands came around front and popped open the top button then reached back again, this time slipping inside the shorts, hands directly on ass — it seemed to please Diesel as he threw his head back and let out a long, "Ahhhhhhhhhh…"

"More?"

Rob's nod came before the word had a chance to come out of his mouth. Diesel's hands slid out of the shorts and made their way to his abs…kneading them slowly and deeply. They then moved up to his leather encased chest. His hands moved in a circular motion, every once in a while, pushing each mass of flesh toward the center.

"More?"

Rob was so turned on, he dipped the camera lens in assent, not wanting to miss a thing by pulling the camera away from his face. Diesel's hands moved down into the front of his shorts caressing the monster within, all the while his hips swaying slowly. Then his hands moved up, stopped for a rub or two on the abs, and on to his chest again, this time underneath the leather casing. His leather-covered hands underneath the leather covering his chest, stretched the material to what seemed its limits. Rob prayed that all the cameras were catching all this.

Diesel looked at the camera in Rob's hands and mouthed, "More?"

Without waiting for an answer, he slipped his hands out from his pecs and quickly popped open the rest of the buttons on his shorts, which promptly fell to his knees. His tool was enormous — with a beautifully shaped extra large head on it. He touched the tip of his dick with a leathered finger, pulled it away so the camera could catch the curved thread of sticky liquid connecting his finger to his dick.

Rob came in his pants. Cumming without touching himself was something Rob hadn't experienced in years. As he slouched backwards in ecstasy, Diesel appeared to be entering the state himself. He grabbed his hardening prick like it was a weed in a garden and began to tug on it. Each tug was accompanied with a grunt. Faster. Faster. Grunts stopped. Focus was on jacking as fast as he could. Rob came to his senses and realized what was happening. As Diesel climaxed, Rob slammed on his shutter release, taking shot after shot in rapid succession. Later, when he developed the film, he realized that he had 14 pictures of Diesel cumming. He could make a mint on each one of them selling them over the net.

Diesel sank to the floor, taking deep breath, while rubbing his leather covered right hand, up and down his right leg, spreading the cum evenly over his muscles.

"Diesel, that's an extra $300. You are the man!" said Rob. Diesel sat on the floor, still rubbing his leg, eyes shut tight, head back with mouth open, gradually coming down from his high. He lifted his glasses onto his head and said, "Sorry for making a mess, Rob, I got kind of carried away."

"Don't worry about it, big guy. It's the kind of mess I don't really mind cleaning up. I'm going out of town for a few days next week. OK with you if we skip a week? Can you come back two weeks from today? That will give me time to show your shots to Casey."

"Works for me. I've got a wrestling tournament next weekend at UT Austin. I can focus on getting ready for it. What do you want me wearing next time?"

"Doesn't matter. Casey'll have something already picked out. Again, probably leather. Sound good to you?"

"Sounds real good. Hey, can I make another deal with you? If this guy Casey ends up getting off on me, rather than on my praising him, can I have a $500 bonus?"

"Sure, Diesel, sure."

Diesel had no idea what was ahead for him. For one thing, he didn't know that Rob had video cameras installed in each of the studio walls. They were on anytime Rob was shooting photos. He'd watch the tapes and decide after each photo shoot if he had good enough stuff to edit into a film to be sold over the net. Most times, it was a bust. Every once in a while, it worked out. And once in a blue moon, it went over the top. Rob watched Diesel's asscheeks kiss each other as he walked to the dressing room to change and all he could see was a blue moon.

"Guy's pretty cute," said Casey as he flipped through the photos of Diesel's first session a week later.

"Take a look at this. I put it together quickly, there's no sound, and the editing needs smoothing out," said Rob as he slipped Diesel's singlet tape into the VCR. Rob was pretty damned proud of what he had already edited together from the 4 different video angles. He figured that he'd end up with about a 25 minute tape he'd sell on the net — already had a name for it — Varsity Stripes.

"Shit! How old is this kid?" said Casey as his eyes widened at Diesel moving around in his singlet.

"He's 23, a senior at A&M, a wrestler. He claims that's the singlet he wrestled in in high school. I kind of doubt it though...but it is a bit snug, wouldn't you say?"

"Snug? The kid might as well be naked. I haven't seen pecs that big since I last looked in a mirror!" Casey laughed, briefly tearing his eyes away from the monitor to glance at Rob. The tape reached the point where the singlet caught under Diesel's pecs. "Those jugs are sweeeeet! His muscles seem to be held together by rubber rather than bones — how can he move that way?"

"He told me that he does yoga to help him focus and with staying flexible," said Rob. Casey made a mental note of that.

Rob was leading Casey right along. He'd invited Casey over for dinner. They were finishing up their second bottle of wine when Rob brought up the subject of a making another film. He knew that Casey would be more agreeable after a relaxed dinner with a healthy amount of wine. Rob was counting on that, and Diesel, to do the trick. Casey's films always sold quite well on the net. He had a small but fiercely loyal following. He always played the father, uncle, scout leader, coach, etc. to some younger male, and abused the guy. Casey hadn't made a film in almost two years. He told Rob that he was getting too old for the business, and it was getting a bit stale for him.

Rob knew that though Casey was nearing 50, he still had a hell of a build on his 6'5" frame. Sure, he wasn't as cut as a Mr. Olympia, but he had mighty nice bulges and recesses in all the right places. And he sure knew how to wrap other guys around his finger...and dick. Rob was hoping that Diesel might trigger an interest in Casey.

The singlet tape finished and Rob slipped in the one of Diesel in leather. Knowing Casey's love of leather (a theme in all his films), Rob hoped the sight of Diesel in some leather would get Casey to commit. "Here's another one, Casey, tell me what you think.

Again, I slapped it together quickly, it needs more editing, there's no sound."

Casey watched the film intently, never moving, never taking his eyes off the monitor.

"I'll do it. That kid. The suit. When?" were all that came out of his mouth as he stood to face Rob at the end of the film. Rob saw a hunger in Casey's eyes he hadn't seen in a while. He also saw Casey's rigid dick snaking down his right leg.

"Next Wednesday? 7?"

"Fine. I think I'll go now, Rob. I'll get here a little early next week and we'll talk things through. I really appreciate all you've done for me over the years...and this...this will be something really good." Casey hugged Rob, kissing him on the side of his neck. Rob enjoyed that massive body pressing on him. Casey's hard-on felt like a police truncheon.

"This is kinda weird, Rob," said Diesel as he held up the black leather body suit that following Wednesday in the dressing room. "Won't this be really hot and uncomfortable?"

"See the zippers all over? They act as tiny air vents. Yes, it will fit pretty tight, but its leather, it will quickly soften with your body heat and you'll barely notice it's on; you move, it moves. Here, I'll help you get into it."

This was turning out better than Rob could have hoped. Casey had been there for over an hour. He was being a bit odd about this shoot, insisting that Diesel and he not see each other till the shoot, going so far as to step out the back door when Diesel arrived, staying there till Rob shuffled Diesel into the dressing room. Rob reminded Casey that as with the other shoots they had done, all the participants knew about the video cameras. Diesel wouldn't know, and believed it was a regular photo shoot.

The "suit" was a full body suit including a hood covering most of the skull. When worn, the only skin visible were hands, feet, mouth and nose, and of course, slits for the eyes. It could be removed sections at a time using the zippers. It had been used only once before, in a film Rob made with Casey a number of years before, with a guy similar in build to Diesel but a bit smaller.

"What are these for?" asked Diesel as he grabbed some hanging tassels while struggling into the outfit.

"They're just decoration," Rob lied. The kid looked good enough to eat! The leather stretched over Diesel's frame looking more like black spray paint. The outfit was tight enough and thin enough that even some of Diesel's more prominent veins could be seen — especially on his arms and legs. The micro-zippers looked like creases in the leather. His white hands and feet looked enormous — his mouth, inviting.

"OK, got the scenario?" asked Rob.

Diesel sighed, "He's my dad, I've come home from football practice, he's upset with me. And I'm supposed to just focus on worshipping him, rubbing him, and shit like that, right?" Diesel spoke absentmindedly, preferring to focus on checking himself out in the mirror. "Fuck, I am hot! That ol' man is gonna be all over me."

"You have no idea, kid, no idea," thought Rob. Out loud he continued, "That's right. Just remember to keep talking. The point is to keep praising him. He really gets off on that — remember that. Though we're only taking pictures, it's real important to him that this play like it's really happening, including all the dialogue — keep imagining in your head that it's a film and not just a photo shoot. The suit comes off in pieces, but don't worry about that. At some point, Casey will probably remove parts of it, just go along with him. By the way, you OK with a bit of spanking?"

"As long as we're playin', he can slap this fine ass all he wants," grinned Diesel as he stood sideways toward the mirror slowly rubbing his firm bulging butt. He faced the mirror and did a double bicep pose along with lifting his straightened right leg while tensing the muscles.

"This is so cool! I'll have this guy drooolin' over me in no time." He tensed his pecs, the hardened masses stretched the leather enough to make it shine even brighter, reflecting the light from above. He rubbed his pecs, impressed that it almost felt like he was touching the skin itself. If anything, the thin leather layer made his skin feel even more sensitive to the touch. Diesel was proud of his chest and loved the way other men drooled over it. He put his hands underneath his pecs and shook them a bit, watching them and the leather ripple. And though his dick impressed just about everybody who saw or felt it, in this outfit, even Diesel was impressed by his crank. At the moment, it was pretty much curled up on itself, stretching and bulging out at the top of his left thigh.

"Remember that we're letting Casey call most of the 'shots' this evening. His bark is much worse than his bite so don't let him shake you up, no matter how much he yels at you — he knows it's a game. He'll pay well for any good pictures I get. He knows that you're OK with the possibility of both of you beating off. I wouldn't worry about it though, Diesel, it usually never happens. And if it does, it just means more cash for you. Any more questions?"

"So I should call him, what, dad, daddy, papa, pops?"

"Yes."

"Hope I can do it with a straight face! What does this Casey look like? Is he some kind of dog who I'll have a hard time pretending to adore?"

"You'll see him for yourself in a minute. I don't think you'll be disappointed. I'll go into the studio and finish setting up. Casey let himself in a while ago. I'll call when we're ready, and you just come in. Remember to treat it as if it were a film, not a photo shoot. And remember to have fun, Diesel!"

Rob left the dressing room. More out of nervousness than anything else, Diesel started doing some calisthenics just to get his blood flowing. About 10 minutes later came the, "OK, Diesel, come on in."

The first thing Diesel noticed was that the studio was more brightly lit than he remembered ever being before.

"Dad? Dad, are you here?" said Diesel, beaming inside with pride for remembering his instructions.

Smack! Diesel staggered a few steps sideways giving his brain the second it needed to realize that he had just been backhanded. His cheek stung, his head was ringing. A split second later he was shoved on the shoulders so hard, he first stumbled backwards, lost his balance, and ended up on the floor on his back, legs spread, propped up on his elbows. A gigantic black leg stepped over his torso, and he looked up to see a Colossus of Rhoads standing over him.

"What the fuck did you do at practice today, you little faggot! Your team was within reach of the winning goal and you fumbled the ball handing it to your quarterback. How the fuck can you fuck that up, when he's got his hands underneath you less than two feet from where the ball is? You're the damned center! Your only job is to bend over, stick your ass in the air, enjoy the quarterback's hands pushin' on your cup, and hand him the ball. And you can't even do that!"

Diesel came out of his mild shock and stared up at this man towering over him, yelling at him. The guy was enormous! He wore black leather chaps, open at the crotch and ass, with black boots. His crotch was covered by some kind of flimsy brief, ass was on full display. His chest was X'd with a leather harness, secured in the middle by a metal ring — same design on back. Diesel noticed the gauntlet gloves and felt the dull throb on his cheek from his first meeting with one of them. Though he had no way to be sure, Diesel guessed that the guy was a good 4 or more inches taller than his own six feet, and he probably outweighed Diesel by at least 40 pounds. And his body was covered with hair — chest was a virtual forest of black hair. Diesel remembered the money and decided to play along, for now.

"Get up!" yelled Casey as he pulled on two of the tassels on the suit, one near each covered ear. Diesel scrambled up, somewhat disoriented from being pulled up by his skull. Casey shoved him against the wall pinning Diesel's shoulders against it with his gloved hands. Casey pressed his crotch into Diesel's, got his face real close and said, "You gotta start doin' better, boy. I'm tired of getting all worked up worrying about how you might fuck things up. I get all agitated and tense." Diesel found himself staring at Casey's eyes. He saw a hunger and a need in them that he'd seen before on other men's eyes, but this time it unnerved him a bit.

Casey just as quickly let go of Diesel, turned and flopped face down on a large foam mat. "Give me one of those rubdowns the coaches give you at school," Casey mumbled as he settled into the mat. Diesel knelt down next to Casey and for the first time examined his body. "This guy really is huge!" thought Diesel, "God, I hope I look half this good when I'm that old." He tentatively put his hands on Casey's back and started to press and rub.

"The oil, asshole, use the oil," growled Casey. Diesel noticed a plastic bottle, squeezed some oil from it onto his hands and went back to Casey's back.

"Harder, Diesel, do it like coach does you."

Diesel put some muscle into it. Casey groaned and began to press his dick into the mat which caused his ass to flex. Diesel couldn't help but stare at Casey's firm exposed ass. He had never seen so much hair on an ass.

"The ass, kid, the ass," said Casey, lifting himself off the matt, looking back at Diesel. Diesel looked at Casey, noticing how Casey's biceps and triceps bulged as he held himself up. He poured more oil onto his hands, never breaking eye contact with Casey, and let his hands find Casey's ass by feel.

"Yeah, that's right...yeah...keep doing that, son."

Without warning, Casey flipped over. Diesel flinched, subconsciously remembering the slap and then immediately getting angry with himself for being fearful. Casey, propped on his elbows, abs tensed, noticed the flinch and smirked, "Don't worry, Diesel, just want to give you more to work on. Get to it, son."

Diesel wanted to show Casey that he wasn't a pushover so he grabbed the bottle of oil, stood up, lifted one leg over Casey's body, and sat down quickly, slamming his ass onto Casey's crotch.

"Thanks, Diesel, that was nice," smiled Casey as he put his gloved hands on Diesel's hips, moving Diesel's body so that it rested nicely on his prick. Diesel poured oil directly onto Casey's chest, tossed the bottle aside, leaned forward and really worked on Casey's chest.

"I'll show this asshole who's in charge!" ran through Diesel's mind as his hands worked over the hairy flesh, slapping over the straps of the leather harness.

Casey knew what Diesel was trying to do, and smiled. "Get down here, Diesel," said Casey as he grabbed Diesel's shoulders and jerked him forward. He put one hand on the top of Diesel's head pushing it so that it landed on his chest, resting on the harness.

"Suck it," instructed Casey as he pressed Diesel's head into his left pec. Diesel started to protest.

"Suck!" was accompanied with smack on Diesel's upraised ass.

Smack! Smack! Smack! Casey slapped Diesel's ass with his right hand as he pulled Diesel's head into his chest, ordering once again, "Suck!"

Diesel obeyed.

"Good boy."

Casey grabbed one of the tassels on the side of Diesel's head and guided Diesel's mouth around his chest. At the same time, he pressed on Diesel's ass with his right hand; till Diesel's leather covered body was pressed against Casey's. He never took his hand off Diesel's hard ass and started to push down on it, jamming Diesel's crotch against his own.

This whole time, Rob was taking picture after picture. He used a zoom mostly because he wanted to stay as much as possible out of range of the hidden video cameras. Sometimes he HAD to get close-ups though. At the moment, he stood near Diesel's feet, seeing Diesel's leather covered body writhing against Casey who had his eyes squeezed shut, mouth hanging open a bit. The V of Diesel's back was almost too perfect to be believed and the way his hips and ass flexed as he pressed into Casey had Rob's dick running with precum.

Casey used both hands to reach for some zippers at the base of Diesel's spine. Diesel didn't notice that he was no longer being forced to slobber on Casey's chest, he just kept it up. Casey pulled a few of the zippers, grabbed Diesel's torso and pushed him back up to a seated position. A gob of spit launched out of Diesel's mouth as he was ripped away from the leather strap he was sucking on. Casey continued with the zippers in the front and ended up removing a section of the suit revealing all of Diesel's lower torso and back. Casey reached for the oil bottle, squeezed a healthy shot toward Diesel's abs, dropped the bottle and started rubbing the oil into Diesel.

"You've been practicing hard, Diesel. These abs are really nice. Daddy likes." He grinned up at Diesel.

As the smooth wet leather gauntlet glove pressed and rolled over his mid-section, Diesel gradually regained his bearings. He started squeezing his ass attempting to pinch Casey's hard rod.

"Let me see your arms, baby," panted Casey as he zipped off more of the suit exposing all of Diesel's arms including most of his shoulders. He also removed a wide section of leather revealing

Diesel's collarbone. Diesel reached for the oil bottle and squeezed some on each shoulder, set down the bottle, held his arms out raised slightly and flexed, and watched the oil run down his arms. Casey began working the oil into Diesel's arms. Diesel could feel Casey flexing his dick over and over.

"Yeah, tables are starting to turn, old man," thought Diesel as he smiled.

"Have I worked hard enough on my chest, daddy?"

Diesel watched Casey's eyes move to leather covered pecs. Diesel slowly flexed and bounced his pecs. Casey seemed transfixed as the micro thin layer of leather stretched over the bulging muscles underneath. Casey's oil slicked gloved hands moved to Diesel's chest. He stretched out his gigantic hands, one on each mass of flesh, but wasn't able to cover either one completely. Casey started to rub them, and squeeze them. Diesel kept his eyes on Casey's eyes, which were glued to Diesel's chest. With his ass, Diesel started squeezing on Casey's steel hard cock in rhythm to the squeezing of his pecs.

Diesel picked up the oil bottle, and as much as he could, pulled the suit away from his body around his neck. He squeezed the bottle four times against his skin and set it down again.

"Go under the leather, daddy. I want to feel you closer," whispered Diesel.

Casey's gloved fingers stopped caressing Diesel's chest and he slid his hands downward. Once low enough, he then slipped his fingertips underneath the leather just above Diesel's abs and moved upward against the hot skin. Halfway up, he had pulled the tight leather away from Diesel's skin enough to let the oil that Diesel had squirted on above, to flow down Diesel's skin and Casey's gloves. Casey spread his fingers like tentacles and began to flex them. All the oil made things very slick under there and it started to run off the edges of his gauntlet gloves. Diesel kept flexing his chest. Casey growled quietly.

"You like them, daddy. Do they make you feel proud of me?"

"Oh, Diesel...my God...you are fucking fantastic..." said Casey through his ragged breathing. He began thrusting his hips upward against Diesel's weight in a fucking motion, his about to explode dick trapped along Diesel's asscrack.

Diesel leaned forward, "Yeah, you like my hot young hard muscled body, don't you, Casey? You want my cum shooter up your hairy ass, don't you? Beg for it, Casey, c'mon, beg!"

"Aaarrrggghhhhh!" bellowed Casey as his hands slid out from the leather. In a flash, Casey lifted Diesel by the waist completely off his body, and reversed their positions — Diesel landed flat on his back on the mat, Casey's ass resting against Diesel's crotch.

Smack! Smack! Smack! Smack! Smack! Smack!

Casey slapped Diesel's leather clad face back and forth, while bouncing fiercely up and down on his crotch. As Diesel was about to cry out in pain, Casey stopped the slapping, covered Diesel's mouth with one hand and wrapped the other around his neck. "Not a sound, bitch, not a sound!" he squeezed out through his gritted teeth.

"Who's Casey? Some sugar daddy who takes care of his little boytoy!!??? No Casey here. You're shit outta luck, muscleboy, shit...out...of...luck."

Diesel's eyes darted around for Rob. He needed to get out of this. He wanted to go. He was scared shitless.

Casey leaned forward bringing his mouth next to one of Diesel's leather covered ears, "And don't even think about calling for Rob. He's not gonna stop me. He's not gonna save you. You are mine and if you don't do what I want, you're gonna be hurtin' for a long time...hurtin' all over...maybe you won't be walking much for a time either. Think about that, fuckboy. All I want is to have a little fun. You're comin' along for the ride, Diesel, you can either have a good time or you can be in agony. You decide, tough guy." The whole time, Casey kept sharply thrusting his ass against Diesel's crotch.

Casey sat up and started manhandling Diesel's pecs. "You got some nice tits on you, boy, real nice. Like huge mounds of Jell-O I can push all over. Flex 'em for me, Diesel, make 'em hard.

"You cryin', Diesel? Aw, don't cry, son. I'm not callin' you a woman. I really like these." Casey pawed at Diesel's chest. Diesel continued quietly crying.

"I said, stop crying, son. Be a man. Do what your daddy wants you to do!"

The sniffling continued. Thud! Thud! Thud! Thud! The sound of leather hitting leather. Casey's fists pounded into Diesel's pecs. "I said, stop crying and tense up those pecs!"

Thud! Thud! Thud! Thud! Thud!

"OK! OK! Stop!" Diesel yelled. Casey stopped. They locked eyes, both sweating and breathing loudly. "Well?" said Casey. Diesel tensed his pecs. Casey gave him a big smile and kneaded the hard muscles.

"Yeah, that's my boy." Casey suddenly leaned down and locked his open mouth onto Diesel's and shoved his tongue in. Diesel felt the tongue move rapidly inside his mouth and held still in terror.

Casey sat back up, bringing his hands back to Diesel's chest. "These are so pretty and soft." Casey untied the front of his chaps with one hand, then ripped off the flimsy brief, soaked with precum and threw them across the room. His dick landed on Diesel's abs with a thud. "Yeah, they are real pretty. Pretty enough to fuck I'd say. What do you think, son?"

Casey grabbed Diesel's chin. "Huh, what do you think?" Casey let go of the chin and lifted his hand sideways in the air.

"Yes! Yes! They are!" yelled Diesel, who just didn't want to get slapped or punched again.

"So glad you agree, baby," said Casey as he slid his hairy ass forward. When the tip of his dick touched the bottom edge of the leather covering Diesel's chest, Casey ordered, "Lift it!"

Diesel looked at Casey perplexed and scared. He didn't want to get hurt and he wanted this to be over but he didn't know what Casey meant.

"Your bra, asshole, lift it and let my log in." Casey chuckled.

Diesel reached up, lifted the edge of the leather, allowing Casey's cock to slip underneath it.

"Thanks, Diesel, I'll make sure you enjoy all this." Casey eased forward till his entire dick was encased in the leather, and rested in the ridge between the two compressed pecs. He slowly pulled back, then moved forward...back...forward..." a ragged sigh exited his throat.

Diesel realized that the hardening dick rubbing back and forth, pressed against his skin, was not an unpleasant feeling.

"Fuck, this feels amazing!" Casey started caressing Diesel's pecs. Just before a thrust, he pressed the two mounds of pec flesh toward each other. His dick was almost completely surrounded by Diesel's flesh. Casey took a sharp intake of air as a shot of pleasure ran through him.

"Diesel, help me. Do this!" Casey grabbed Diesel's hands and slammed them onto the leather-covered mounds.

"Press 'em together, boy."

Diesel pressed his hands toward each other, bunching his pecs. Casey fell forward, his hands landing on the mat well above Diesel's head. The flesh surrounding his dick sent shocks of pleasure through his whole body. He started fucking faster...and faster...

"Push harder, mother fucker, harder!" screamed Casey. His whole focus was on getting off. He needed to shoot cum. He ached to shoot cum. He let all his weight land on Diesel, focusing on the fuck alone. The center ring of his harness rubbed back and forth along and past Diesel's forehead. Lucky for Diesel he had the leather hood on which protected his skin from being ripped up. Casey's hairy hard abs moved back and forth over Diesel's open mouth. Diesel was caught up in the sexual frenzy himself. He kept his mouth open and pressed his tongue along Casey's abs as they traveled back and forth.

Casey suddenly lifted his upper body off of Diesel and looked down at himself powerfucking Diesel's chest. The leather top had bunch up enough that with each thrust forward, Casey's dick peeked out of the top and was within inches of Diesel's chin. Casey ripped at a zipper on Diesel's jaw and jerked the leather hood off Diesel's head. Seeing Diesel's prettyboy face caused Casey to once again lock lips with him. This time, Diesel's tongue hungrily wrestled back.

Casey pulled his mouth away. "Here it comes, fuckboy!" shouted Casey as he pushed forward one last time. Casey's cum shot out in volleys as he bellowed like a bull. A couple of spurts sprayed out on either side of Diesel's head. Three more landed on his face and hair. The rest dribbled out and collected in the depression near Diesel's neck.

For about 30 seconds, Casey and Diesel just stared at each other breathing fiercely. Casey's sweat dripped all over Diesel. Casey sat back up and began massaging Diesel's scalp, rubbing his cum into it. "That was real good, son, I'm proud of you."

"Thanks...dad...," said Diesel tentatively, trying to figure out what rules were in place at the moment.

Casey leaned down, kissed Diesel's cheek and moved over to his ear. "On to Act 2, my little grasshopper," and then explored Diesel's ear with his tongue. Diesel moaned. He was tired, but more relaxed than he'd been in a while. Casey worked his way down Diesel's body stopping at his belly button. He started biting Diesel's treasure trail and pulling on the hairs. He jerked hard on a zipper that opened Diesel's leather pants in half front to back, exposing his fat joint, balls and asshole.

"You're a big boy all over, Diesel," said Casey staring jealously at a cock that was as long as it was fat. It looked like a fireplug, a tall, fat fireplug. He started slobbering all over it, moved on to the balls sucking them in one at a time, rolling his tongue around them. Diesel just kept up his moaning. Casey's tongue slipped below the balls brushing against Diesel's pucker.

"Don't," Diesel froze.

Casey looked up at Diesel, his eyes burning with sudden anger. He shoved an index finger into Diesel's asshole with a grunt.

"Aaaaaiiiiiiiiiiiaaaaaaaa!" came out of Diesel's throat as he sat up and attempted to grab Casey. The veins in Diesel's neck looked like they were about to pop and from the neck up he was turning bright red. Casey locked onto Diesel's neck with his free hand and squeezed cutting off Diesel's air supply.

"What did you say?" he asked incredulously. "Did you tell me not to do THIS?" he yelled as he pushed his finger in harder and wiggled it. "You don't ever tell me what not to do, Diesel, EVER."

Just before it looked like Diesel was going to pass out, Casey let go of his neck with a shove. Diesel fell back on the mat, gasping for breath. He forgot for a moment that something was squirming in his asshole. Casey yanked his finger out of its hot enclosure, scooted forward holding Diesel's arms down, and rubbed the tip of his dick in Diesel's trench.

"Yes, Diesel, you're going to have a visitor. He's gonna come in, leave you a present, and then leave. He's at the door, guy, you gonna let him in or is he gonna have to break down the door? It's your choice, son."

Diesel was actually shaking with fear. He kept telling himself that this was just not happening. And then he'd feel that leaking piece of steel at his asshole. Casey brought his mouth down to Diesel's ear again and said, as if he could read Diesel's mind, "This is happening whether you like it or not. We can both enjoy it, or just me. If you want to, you know what to do. Knock, knock, you big jock," Casey laughed.

Diesel looked around, thinking that he'd see or find a way out of this. But there was nothing. He looked up at Casey's face as it dripped sweat on him.

"You're just so fine, Diesel. Let me make you feel good. Let me in, boy!" Casey kept hitting Diesel's asshole. Diesel relented for a second and Casey felt the head of his dick slip in. Diesel screamed in pain. Casey covered Diesel's mouth with his, feeling the strong vibrations of the screaming. It really turned Casey on. He kept pushing harder and harder, slowly sinking into a tight tight inferno. He hit bottom. They both froze. Casey started to pull out very slowly. He couldn't believe that it was almost as difficult to pull out as it was to push in.

"Christ, this kid is tight!" he thought. He pushed in again...pulled out...in...out. Casey took his mouth off of Diesel's but kept his faces inches from Diesel's.

"Please...no...it hurts," choked Diesel.

"Please...yes...," whispered Casey. "Relax, kid, relax," said Casey as he continued his smooth ins and outs.

Diesel suddenly jerked. "Ugh!" came out of his mouth.

"That was your prostate. Feels good, doesn't it? Here, I'll hit it again...and again."

Diesel was still in pain, but these sudden jolts of pleasure made the pain feel almost pleasant. Casey straightened up, let go of Diesel's arms and grabbed a leg in each hand. He started fucking Diesel a little faster and with this slight change in angle, he discovered that more of his dick hit Diesel's prostate. He also noticed that Diesel's dick was shifting around and starting to straighten out while resting on Diesel's abs.

"The kid is enjoying this! Fuck, I knew this little cocksucker was a born bottom!" thought Casey.

This was another moment where Rob felt the need to get some close-ups with his camera. He shot over Casey's shoulder, getting all of Diesel down to where Casey pounded in and out of him. Diesel was a mess, covered with sweat — cum and sweat mixed on the wet leather now barely covering his chest. He was taking big gulps of air punctuated with Casey's thrusts. His long wet blonde hair also shook with each push. Casey had Diesel's legs by the ankles. He started pushing the legs outward.

"C'mon, spread 'em for me, Diesel" Casey ordered as he continued his assault. Both Casey and Rob were amazed at how flexible Diesel's legs were — that yoga must be something. Diesel's legs ended up almost parallel to the ground.

"I'm gettin' there, Diesel. Like it? Oh, yeah, you like it. Your dick tells me you like it. Your ass is so hot, you got my dick feelin' like a piece of hot steel...oh, Diesel!" Casey yelled as Diesel squeezed his ass muscles. "Do that again, Diesel, do it for daddy." He did. And again. And again.

Casey lost control and turned into a pile driver. Diesel rocked his head back and forth. He reached forward and grabbed the top of Casey's chaps. "Fuck me, daddy...fuck me, Casey...fuck me!"

Casey pulled out and started shooting cum in the air. Rob told him days later that his first two shots landed almost six feet beyond Diesel's head. He had to show Casey the video to prove it to him. Ropes of cum landed in rows along Diesel's muscled body. By the time Casey stopped shooting, there was cum everywhere and the smell was overpowering.

Casey was getting tired, but he had one more thing to do to make sure this cocky kid was broken in. He dragged Diesel off the mat, sat down on a weight bench sideways, pulling the limp musclekid's body onto his lap, both facing a large mirror on the wall. He zipped the top piece of leather off Diesel, and leered as he watched Diesel's massive pecs hang over his abs. He wrapped one arm around Diesel's stomach, started kneading Diesel's dick with the other.

"OK, Diesel, this is it. You're gonna cum for me. Keep looking in the mirror."

Casey made sure that Diesel could feel his dick on Diesel's ass as it rested in Casey's lap. He kept yanking on Diesel's prick, sometimes doing a twisting motion. All the while he whispered in Diesel's ear, "Look at your body, Diesel. You are so fuckin' muscular. Look at the veins in your arms...you can see the blood pulsing through them. Your shoulders, Diesel, see how huge and wide they are. Abs... watch them move as you breathe. And that chest...that chest...," Casey stuck his tongue in Diesel's ear.

"Play with your chest, Diesel, play," he whispered.

Diesel wasn't really listening to Casey. Some individual words slipped into his brain. He saw a muscular body in front of him with a huge dick being jacked. He saw a huge set of pecs and wanted to touch them. Suddenly, he was touching them. He rubbed them and pushed them around. He found the nipples, hard, pointed. He pulled on them. He pulled hard. His head fell backward. Suddenly he jerked his head forward. The dick in the mirror was huge. A gloved hand moved up and down the rigid column. The column seemed to suddenly expand. The hand almost lost its grip. Diesel's eyes widened, he stopped breathing. Suddenly he let out a great whoosh of air from his lungs, looked upward as he realized someone was dropping gobs of what felt like warm syrup all over him. He passed out.

Diesel opened his eyes and could make out two figures through his hazy vision. He felt weak and tired.

"I'll have the film in a couple of weeks. Casey, it will be your best ever. I can't thank you enough. And you thought this was getting stale for you."

"Hey, this kid almost killed me. But it was worth it. I can't believe how fuckin' hot he is. Think he'd ever do this again?"

"I don't know. My guess is he's kinda new to all this. Hey, look, he's comin' round."

Casey moved toward the prone figure of Diesel. "Hey, little buddy, how ya feelin'?"

Diesel tried to talk but nothing came out. He felt so exhausted but he wanted something.

"What is it, Diesel? What are you trying to say?" as Casey moved closer to Diesel, putting his ear near Diesel's mouth.

"More..." came out in a light breath from Diesel.

"What?"

"More...more...," whispered Diesel. He grabbed at Casey's arm. Casey easily pushed him away.

"Get some fuckin' sleep, kid."

"Kid's mumbling something...doesn't make sense. Guess you should let him sleep here till morning. I'll see ya in a couple of weeks, Rob."

Casey took a final look at the sleeping naked Diesel. Even after the grueling workout Casey took him through, he looked magnificent. "That kid is a total package," he thought, and walked out.

A Boner Book

CHAPTER 5

The Coaches

Texas A&M football coach Jim Erickson sat perched on the edge of his desk, legs spread, staring with lust filled eyes at the massive football player standing in front of him as his hands reached for the player's hips. He gripped the dirt smudged football player's pants and pulled Diesel forward, his hungry open mouth attacking Diesel's.

He'd taken his varsity team through a pretty grueling workout that afternoon. Now that the team had gotten their aggression out slamming into each other, piling on each other, pushing and rubbing against each other, Coach E needed to re ease his.

Diesel had followed the usual plan of pretending to want some extra practice alone and stayed on the field. By the time he sauntered into the locker room, the other players were gone. With helmet in hand, he headed toward the coach s office knowing that Coach E would be inside pacing with anticipation.

Diesel reminded the coach of his son Jim Jr. who'd graduated a year before Diesel's arrival four years before. Jim Jr. held more than half of the current football records at Texas A&M. He was now in grad school. Though strongly attracted to his son, Coach E had been able to hold himself back.

But Diesel was too much for him. Diesel's hard muscled smooth body, topped with curly blonde hair, made the coach see his son just about every time he caught a glimpse of Diesel. Coach E had been able to wait for Diesel to hit 21 in the Spring of his junior year before acting on his needs.

He knew Diesel would never be the spectacular player his son was, after all, the sport Diesel really excelled in was wrestling; he was built wider and taller than Jim Jr. Coach E realized that no kid he'd ever coached had the body that Diesel carried.

Diesel had known for years that other men were attracted to him and that sometimes the need seemed stronger in older men. Soon after his sessions started with Coach E, Diesel turned the tables by videotaping one of their sessions with a hidden camera. With the threat of exposure hanging over his head, Coach E agreed to be the "teacher" for two Independent Studies Diesel signed up for each semester of his senior year, guaranteeing an A+ in each, pumping up Diesel's GPA respectably. Diesel agreed to continue the sex, mainly because he really enjoyed it. He got off on the fact that coach loved the rough sex between them and he didn't have to do much at all. And the coach seemed to get off on how Diesel did his role playing in their heated sexual encounters.

"The jersey, kid" said the sweating coach as he broke the kiss and reached behind him for the baby oil. Diesel pulled the jersey off and tossed it on the couch. Coach E poured some oil on one hand and began rubbing it into Diesel's abs. Diesel tensed his abs; coach rubbed harder in response, "That's it Junior, make 'em hard!" He poured more oil, rubbed his meaty hands together, pulled Diesel into another sloppy kiss, and began rubbing his hands over Diesel's muscled back. He shoved his hands up under the shoulder pads and then down underneath Diesel's tight pants, far enough to feel the curve of Diesel's butt as it expanded outward. Coach E groaned into Diesel's mouth and pulled Diesel's ass toward him.

"Coach is hornier than usual," thought Diesel as the coach fumbled with the strings of Diesel's football pants. Diesel could see the bald spot forming on coach's head as the coach concentrated on getting to his prize. Diesel thought that for an old man somewhere in his mid- 50's, Coach Erickson was in really good shape. He was a couple of inches shorter than Diesel's 6', but really firmly built. Diesel sensed that though coach was pretty hot now, in his day, he must have been a really hot catch. Diesel grunted as he realized the humor in that thought, "Yes, Coach E certainly is a catcher and not a pitcher," rolled through his mind. Coach didn't even notice the small chuckle.

The coach slid off the desk onto his knees as he slobbered over Diesel's hard protective cup, having finally unlaced the pants and yanked them down to Diesel's mid-thighs. Diesel rubbed the back of coach's head as the coach gnawed away with a low growl at the hard plastic.

"Daddy, you lookin' for something?" asked Diesel.

Coach E was getting more frenzied. He could feel Diesel's enormous package moving along with the cup he chewed and lapped on. The rich aroma of sweaty dirty musclecock filled his nostrils. Pulling away slowly, he reached for the top of the jockstrap and put his fingers under the elastic on top. Instead of pulling the waist down, he ran his hands back and forth following the curve of Diesel's waist. The bottoms of his fingers ran along the wet lumpy material of the strap, the tops of his fingers moving along Diesel's smooth hot skin. He had learned to savor moments like this.

"Coach, I got chores to do at home," said Diesel, breaking the "game" but eager to get his nut off and get home. Coach E pulled the jockstrap down angrily and watched Diesel's dick and balls spring upward and then bounce heavily downward, almost in slow motion.

Coach's anger floated away as he got that same thrill every time he watched Diesel's massive package take a defiant stand once freed; he loved fantasizing about his son having a cock the size of this god in front of him. Diesel's balls churned in anticipation of a workout; the oversized tube of meat, marbled with veins that coach was sure no painter could ever reproduce faithfully, hung downward, causing the churning balls to move into position like two altar boys standing obediently next to a tall priest.

"Mmmmmmmmmm," came out of coach's mouth over and over as he moved his lips around Diesel's dick and balls. Diesel was always amazed at how much saliva Coach E produced. But then again, if he didn't, Diesel wouldn't half enjoy fucking the coach's mouth as much as he did. Mouth? No, Diesel didn't fuck Coach E's mouth, he fucked the coach's throat.

It was time. Coach E stood and lay down lengthwise on his desk on his back, scooting so his head hung off the edge. He looked up at Diesel and as always, savored the upside down sight of Diesel's meaty pecs, pressed on by the shoulder pads strapped to his body. Coach E reached for them as Diesel's hardening cock aimed for the hot wet mouth begging to be entered.

By the time Diesel had just his dickhead in Coach E's mouth, he was already choking a bit. This always happened. Diesel reached forward to rub the coach's rippled firm stomach.

"C'mon pops, lemme in. Just relax. Let junior in to make a deposit," purred Diesel as he shoved his dick further into the furnace of a mouth. He winced in pain as he felt coach pulling on his nipples, knowing that this also helped coach relax his throat.

Then came Diesel's favorite part. He focused on the photo on the office wall of Assistant Football Coach Anthony Cimino. Coach C was in his second year at the school, 31, 6'2" of hot hard and hairy prime Italian stock. The photo was taken in college just after Coach C had been named All State Tight End at U of Oklahoma. The camera caught him in midair, ball in hand, with a huge smile on his face. He was helmetless, wavy black hair freeze framed in motion, wearing a cropped practice jersey flapping up in the wind showing off the mass of dark hair on his stomach. Between the bottom of the cotton shorts and the tops of his striped socks, his legs were covered with thick curly black hair. Though the hair hid some of the definition, you could tell he had very powerful legs. And though it could have been the wind or a trick of the camera lens, the photo also showed a sizable mound inside the shorts.

"C'mon, daddy, open up...give it up," panted Diesel as he stared at Coach C's crotch in the photograph. He'd been doing this long enough with Coach E that he knew what really got the coach off was having his air supply cut off by Diesel's huge dick in his mouth. Diesel had never been able to get his whole dick in Coach E's mouth; so far he'd met very few mouths and throats big enough to do that. But he'd pump in and out of Coach E's throat, letting streams of coach's saliva run out of his mouth each time he pulled out, and causing a tensing of coach's body each time he shoved back in till stopped by his own girth. They'd tried different ways and Diesel realized he could stuff the most of his sausage into Coach E's mouth while the coach was on his back with his head hanging.

Diesel put his body on autopilot as he daydreamed about sex with Coach Cimino. He'd never seen Coach C in the buff, but had seen enough parts at different times to know that there probably wasn't a place on his body without some hair, and that made Diesel really hot. He also knew that Coach C had kept the hard muscled body that got him named All State. When Coach Cimino had first arrived, Coach Erickson would sometimes, but not often enough for Diesel's needs, have Coach C practice with the guys, rotating positions. Diesel really liked it each time Coach C slapped him on the ass, or rubbed the back of his neck after he'd made some great play.

Diesel was drawn back to reality as he senses his impending climax. He glanced down to see that Coach E had already cum, the stain on his shorts gradually expanding. He also sensed that Coach E had passed out. But Diesel knew he had time so he furiously fucked Coach E's mouth and throat. With each forward thrust he panted out, "Tony!" while staring at the photo.

He came in great torrents as usual. He felt his cum shooting into Coach E's throat and mouth. Some of his massive load worked its way into Coach E's nasal passages and came out his nose, seeping into Diesel's pubes.

Diesel pulled out, the tip of his dick tumbling down Coach E's nose and forehead as his head hung off the desk. He lifted Coach E's head and started slapping each side of his face. "Coach, wake up, wake up, its time to go," said Diesel. Coach E came to life suddenly, choking. He got off the desk, leaned forward, and spit out strings of saliva mixed with lumps of Diesel's cum. Diesel put his jersey back on and headed for the locker room. Coach E watched Diesel's ass, with the tight material of the pants painted onto the hard glutes, move slowly and sensually away.

A week later, Coach Erickson broke his leg in 3 places in a freak accident tripping down the bleachers in one of the gyms. He had emergency surgery and found out he'd be in traction for at least 2 weeks, then start physical therapy which could include a number of weeks on a crutch. He was OK, but not happy about being away from his Aggies.

The rest of the faculty split up Coach Erickson's job, Tony Cimino took over as head football coach. He had a degree in Sports Physiology and was an accomplished masseuse. At first he was a bit scared about taking over as head coach but quickly eased into the responsibilities, eager to prove to Coach Erickson that when he returned, he'd find his team in top shape and spirits. Tony went out of his way to keep the team working hard and in good spirits.

"Thanks, guys," Diesel grunted as two of his team mates helped him sit down on the padded table in the coach's office. He'd pulled something right near the end of practice and had doubled over in pain on the field. Coach Cimino got the two guys to help Diesel into the office so he could check to see if Diesel needed to go to the hospital.

Diesel sat on the table in full uniform swearing to himself for getting hurt. Coach Cimino bounded in the office, set down his clipboard on the desk, and walked over to Diesel. "So what happened out there, Diesel?" he asked as he put a hand on Diesel's shoulder and walked around to face him.

"I'm not sure, Coach C. I was going back to catch a pass, turned to my right and then, whammo, my leg hurt like a son of a gun and I fell over." Diesel focused on the mound of black curly hair spilling out of the "v" of the unbuttoned short sleeve red polo shirt that Coach C was wearing.

"Does it still hurt? Where? What kind of pain was it?"

"Here...and yes, it still does," said Diesel as he put his hand high up inside his right thigh. "I just remember it was some kind of a sharp pain. It doesn't hurt as much now, but I can feel it."

"Sorry, Diesel, didn't mean to hurt you," said Coach C as he pulled his hand away from Diesel's leg following Diesel's jerk. The touch hadn't really hurt; Diesel was just surprised finding this Italian stud's hand within millimeters of his dick.

"That's OK, Coach, it didn't hurt that much. Do I have to go to the hospital?"

"I can't really tell without seeing your leg. Can we take a look?"

"Sure!" Coach Cimino squatted down and began untying and removing Diesel's cleats. Diesel couldn't help but admire Coach C's ass that he spotted by looking over coach's head as he bent over Diesel's feet. He was wearing those dumb polyester stretch shorts that lots of coaches wore, but they looked mighty fine wrapped around this paisano. Diesel worked at the laces at his waist, remembering the countless times Coach Erickson had done the same thing.

Diesel held his body up using his arms pressed against the padded table top while Coach C pulled his pants down to just above Diesel's knees.

"Coach Erickson told me you were the strongest guy on the team and I think you just proved it by holding yourself up in the air like that. Those are some pretty big guns you've got there, Diesel," said Coach C as he put a hand on each of Diesel's upper arms.

"Thanks, coach...nice of you to notice," said Diesel with a slight blush.

"Now let me see," said Coach Cimino as his fingertips started gently moving around Diesel's upper leg, "let me know when it hurts a lot." Diesel stared at Coach Cimino's hands as they poked and prodded his skin, and moved so close to his jockstrap. One hand brushed the jockstrap, Diesel let out a grunt.

"Did that hurt?" asked the coach with a look of concern.

"No, no, I was just clearing my throat."

"I think I may know what the problem is. Can I get you to lay down on the table?" asked the coach as he helped Diesel get his legs up on the table and pulled the football pants completely off. Diesel laid there in full football gear from the waist up, minus the helmet, and with only a jockstrap on from the waist down. On top of it, Diesel realized that it was one of his oldest jockstraps. So old, that where the pouch connected to the waistband in front, the material was quite frayed and barely connected. Usually when one of his jocks got this beat up, Diesel saved it to wear on special occasions when he was out on the prowl for sex with another guy, or dancing for money in some club. Sometimes, a guy would pay him a lot of money for one of his beat up old jocks after he'd cum in it. He hadn't paid attention to the sad shape this jock was in when he whipped it on before practice. The advantage to an old jockstrap though was that his oversized dick and balls didn't feel as constricted in the loose pouch. His dick was lying kind of sideways in the jockstrap.

Diesel couldn't see over his shoulder pads but could feel Coach Cimino's hands working in the cleft of his right leg and crotch. One of coach's hands started bumping regularly into Diesel's nutsack, and brushing along his cock. Diesel started to get hard. He could feel his dick slowly moving northward. He felt it lifting up stretching the frayed material by the waiststrap. He started breathing more quickly realizing that he was getting closer to a climax faster than just about anytime before in his life.

"Coach!" yelled Diesel.

"Huh? Am I hurting yo....wha??!!!??" yelled Coach Cimino as Diesel's rock hard dick ripped through the few remaining pieces of fabric holding the pouch to the waist of the jock, and sprayed volley after volley of cum all over Diesel's jersey, with one shot going as far as his forehead.

Diesel sat up, breathless, "Coach, I am so sorry!" as he stared horrified at Coach Cimino. Coach C was staring at Diesel's rock hard cock, sticking up at a 45 degree angle, looking more like a salami from his uncle's butcher shop than a dick. It was huge! "I think it's bigger than my own!" thought Tony.

"No, Diesel, I'm the one who's sorry. I was so focused on massaging your muscle that I didn't see anything. This was all my fault. You're a young guy and can get hard when the wind blows on your dick! I've embarrassed you and am very very sorry. I should have been more professional."

Diesel hopped off the table, ignoring the slight pain in his leg, and started wiping his jersey off with some towels lying around. He then pulled the jersey off over his head, and continued wiping the cum juice off his now hanging dick, the shredded pouch hanging below it. Then he pulled his football pants on, leaving them unlaced.

As he picked up the rest of his gear and started to head for the locker room, Coach C, grabbed one of his muscled forearms, "Diesel, wait." He used a Kleenex to wipe the gob of cum still stuck to Diesel's forehead into which a curl of his blonde hair had stuck. "You'd have a hard time explaining that to the rest of the guys," he said with a smile.

Diesel half smiled at the coach and left the office. Tony watched him leave, with the image of the huge cock ripping through the jockstrap in his mind. He brought the Kleenex to his nose, took a whiff, and then threw it in the garbage can.

A week later, leg fully recovered and feeling a lot more relaxed and cocky around Coach Cimino, Diesel was indulging himself by showering in the coach's private stall in his office. Coach Erickson had been letting Diesel use it when he wanted, and Coach Cimino didn't mind any of the team members using it. Though it was a junior varsity practice day, Diesel had spent the afternoon working with free weights, ending with a 30 minute run on a treadmill. His muscles ached from the workout, but it was that deep satisfying ache Diesel knew meant that his body was taking care of itself, growing more and hardening more.

He'd beaten off plenty of times at home the past week going over the sensations he felt while Coach C had worked on his leg and envisioning his hairy body. He'd finished soaping up and was now just letting the hot water ripple over his hard muscles, washing the suds down the drain. Thoughts of Coach Cimino naked and begging Diesel to fuck him entered Diesel's mind; he began soaping his cock, feeling it harden and extend. Suddenly the office door opened.

"Hey, who's in my shower? I stink and need to get myself unstunk!" yelled Coach C good naturedly. He spotted Diesel's wet head since the glass shower door was only 5' high. "Well, if it isn't my favorite hot spring!" When it was just the two of them the coach and Diesel had fallen into a pattern of joking about what had happened the previous week, though there was always an edge of tension in their wordplay. It worked better for both of them rather than just ignoring what had happened. "Warn me if an eruption will happen when you come out!"

Diesel turned the water off, wrapped a towel around his waist and stepped out of the shower. He was taken aback seeing Coach Cimino sweaty, muddied and suited up in full football gear. He hadn't seen Coach C in full gear since the last time he scrimmaged with the varsity players at the end of the previous season.

"What's the occasion? Trying out for JV football, coach?" Diesel asked as he started drying himself off, trying to convince himself that he was not that aroused by the sight. Tony set his helmet on a file cabinet and walked toward the desk, cleats sounding on the floor, while staring at Diesel's cut body. "And he's got the dick of death. Life's just not fair!" thought Tony, smiling to himself.

"Every once in a while, it's a good idea for a coach to scrimmage with his team. I play a lot more often with the JV's rather than you varsity guys because they're a better team," said Coach C, hoping to get a rise out of Diesel.

"Right...better...," said Diesel with a sly smile and a wink.

Coach C leaned against the desk, unlaced his cleats, and pulled them and his socks off.

"Gee, Coach, you've got hair everywhere, even on your feet!"

"Well, there's not much I can do about it. It all started appearing in junior high and shows no sign of retreating...anywhere. I used to be embarrassed about it, but not any more," said Coach C, now sitting on the edge of the desk, the same edge Coach E's head hung off during all those skull fuckings Diesel gave him. He brought one leg up on the desk and started massaging his calf. Diesel mentally saw Coach C's asshole winking in anticipation of Diesel's entry in place of Coach E's mouth.

"Embarrassed? How could you be embarrassed about being hairy? I always wished I had more hair. This blonde stuff I've got is nothing," said Diesel, noting the thickness of the black hair on coach's calf.

"Hair isn't always a blessing, my young friend. Lots of people are turned off by it. My fiancée, has made me promise that I'll get my back waxed before our honeymoon! It can clog up a drain. Why, and don't tell this to anyone, I've even caught hair in the zipper of my jeans more than once — and that can cause quite a jolt if you're not paying attention! And going to the beach can cause a lot of staring. No, hairy is no bed of roses, my friend." Diesel slowed down his towel movement as he pictured Coach Cimino zipping up a pair of old tight jeans trying to make sure no hair gets caught. His dick twitched, already half hard from the aborted launch in the shower and seeing Coach C's ass resting where Coach E's neck had hung...many times. He had no idea that at the same time, Coach C was thinking about how amazing Diesel's almost hairless muscled body looked.

"Besides, no body hair lets all your muscles show. Look at you! If you were covered with hair, no one would be able to see how terrific your body is, Diesel — and what you've got is something to be proud of...real proud. Be glad you don't have this," said Coach C as he lifted his dirty jersey revealing his taut stomach, covered with black hair half stuck to his skin with sweat.

"Well, I think hair on a guy is sexy...I mean...I know lots of girls here who think you're the hottest guy in the school, coach. Besides, there's nobody here who doesn't know what good shape you're in, coach, no matter how much hair you think is hiding things!" said Diesel as he snapped his towel at Coach C's calf and laughed. Coach C grabbed at the snapping towel, instead hooking onto the one around Diesel's waist, and pulled it off. They stood looking at each other for a moment in shock. Tony's eyes bore into Diesel's fat cock as it slowly swayed.

"Warning, warning, ICBM missile spotted hovering in the coach's office," said Tony as he grabbed his helmet, slid off the desk and ducked behind a chair. Diesel just started laughing, glad coach found a way to ease the situation. He grabbed the pump bottle of skin lotion Coach Erickson kept on his desk, squirted some into his hands, and began rubbing it into his left leg.

"It surprises me the way guys will find some things that are good for them completely repulsive, and yet accept others with ease," said Coach C as he stood back up leaving the helmet on the floor, watching Diesel applying the lotion to his skin, realizing that he found the sight pretty arousing. "Using a skin lotion right after a shower is the best way to keep your skin hydrated. Why in God's name would you actually choose to accept that as a good thing to do, Diesel, why? You're a college kid. Your job is to pay no attention to your elders."

"Good? I do it cuz I like the way it makes my skin shine!" chuckled Diesel, "let's all those muscles you talk about stand out...see?" Diesel extended his leg and tensed the muscle. He squirted more lotion on his hands and began working on his left thigh. "Hydrate? What's a hydrate?" he grinned. Tony had a hard time not staring at Diesel's body as his muscles moved sensuously under his skin as he continued to rub cream into himself.

Tony knew that Diesel was pulling his leg, but he was starting to feel vaguely uncomfortable with a naked hot musclestud in front of him. He figured it was time to jump in the shower — maybe Diesel would be done "shining" himself and gone by the time he got out. He stepped out from behind the desk, and pulled off his jersey, dropping it on the floor. As he began unsnapping his shoulder pads, his back was to Diesel. Diesel stopped rubbing his leg and stared at Coach C's back. He'd never seen hair covering so much of a guy's back — and he found it incredibly hot. He noticed coach's arm and back muscles work as he worked to remove the shoulder pads. Coach C was a couple of inches taller than Diesel, and it sure looked to Diesel like coach had wider shoulders than he did. He drank in coach's hot ass encased in the football pants and wondered about his package up front. Diesel was getting hard.

"Would you get my back, coach?" asked Diesel quietly, having walked up to the musclebound Italian who was now half dressed. Tony had just unlaced his pants and turned around to Diesel, a bit surprised to see a massive back about a foot in front of him. All kinds of danger signs went off in Tony's brain. Here he was, an adult, a coach, a teacher — half naked alone in his office, the door shut, and a naked guy, a kid, a student — asking to be touched. Tony shook off his fear and grabbed the lotion. "What the hell, he's asking for my help," he reasoned to himself.

Diesel's hot skin quickly warmed up the cool lotion Tony had pumped onto his hands. As he rubbed the lotion around, replenishing more than once, Tony automatically went into massage mode — his training caused that. But massage training didn't tell him to enjoy running his hands over the smooth mountainous back as much as he was. He worked Diesel's shoulders hard. Diesel let out a small sound with a sigh. Tony stared at the back of Diesel's head. He could tell Diesel's neck was relaxed. The blonde curls on Diesel's head swayed in rhythm to Tony's movements. Tony was getting hard.

"Coach, you got the best hands. Nobody's ever made my muscles feel this good," said Diesel, almost in a whisper. Sweat had broken out on Tony's forehead. His hands moved, almost on their own will, to Diesel's arms. He took a step forward to grip them better. Looking down, he noticed the loose laces of his pants brushing against Diesel's bubble butt. He also noticed Diesel tense his ass cheeks — more than once.

"My back...again...please," said Diesel as he bent forward slightly. Tony got more lotion and rubbed Diesel's shoulder blades. Diesel's bare ass was now pressing against the shiny material covering Tony's crotch.

Tony was completely hard, and leaking, but he knew Diesel would have no idea of that since he had his pants on and his support cup was in place.

Diesel could sense that Tony was aroused by his breathing — deep and a little ragged. He stood up and slowly turned his naked body to face the coach, his dick noticeably longer and jutting outward.

"Do my front, coach, I'm tense...please," Diesel focused his blue eyes on Tony's brown eyes. Tony's hands dropped to his side. He wanted to stop...desperately. Diesel picked up the bottle of lotion, squirted two pumps, slowly, onto each of his own pecs, set the bottle down, and placed each of Tony's hands on a pec. "Do me, coach...do me."

Tony again went into massage mode and worked Diesel's pecs. They were meaty enough that working on them while standing was a real pleasure. Diesel would tense them to hardness, causing

Tony to work harder, then he'd relax them. Each time he relaxed, both men moaned quietly.

Diesel picked up the bottle of lotion, unscrewed the top, and poured a liberal amount into one of his hands. Setting the bottle down, he poured some of the lotion into his other hand, then slapped both of them onto Tony's hairy stomach and immediately started working the lotion into the hair, pleasantly surprised to find the hair soft and silky. He could feel the coach's hard abs under the mat of hair. He moved his hands in circular wet motions lower...and lower.

"Please, Diesel...no...don't...please," pleaded Tony, helpless to stop things.

"Please...yes...that's what I want to do, coach...please you," whispered Diesel, his face now inches from Tony's. Tony continued massaging Diesel's pecs, focusing on Diesel's nipples, without realizing it, he started to gently tug and squeeze them. Diesel forced Tony's pants completely open in front and pulled them down slightly. He next pulled the plastic cup of the jockstrap off and tossed it aside. He grabbed the bottle of lotion, pulled out the waistband of Tony's jock, and dumped in some lotion. Tony hissed and his hands froze on Diesel as the cool lotion seeped onto his rock hard cock through the thick pubic hair. Diesel quickly put the bottle down and jammed his hands into the jockstrap, squishing the lotion into the mass of hair, and onto what he was pleased to discover, was an oversized Italian cum gun. He worked it slowly into an up position.

"Oh, yeah, this guy's got a dick on him!" thought Diesel.

Diesel's own dick was cocked and ready to go. He stepped closer to the coach, panting face to face, pulled the pouch of the jockstrap open on the side, and slipped his dick in. The two torpedoes pulsed next to each other. Primal instincts took over as they pressed their crotches together, locked mouths, and wrapped their arms around each other. Diesel's slick hands coated Tony's back hair as he slowly moved his hands on the coach's back. Their tongues angrily dueled.

The men rutted. Each moved toward his own goal. The other man was a tool used to reach the end zone. They broke the kiss and again, on instinct, moved their heads to each other's left and locked their mouths onto each other's necks. Tony moaned and spit saliva. Diesel bit.

The bite caused Tony to reach the goal post first. He howled as he shot his first round. As he pulsed more and more cocksnot, Diesel joined, adding an even larger amount of warm cum to the mix. Tony's jockstrap was completely soaked in cum.

After about 30 seconds of gradually slowed down breathing, Diesel slid his hands into the back of Tony's loose pants, cupping a hard and, he was pleased to discover, hairy ass. He moved his sweaty face so that he was facing his coach.

"Coach... coach...Tony?" said Diesel as he gripped Tony's chin. Tony stared at Diesel, like a deer in headlights. "OK if I call you Tony...Tony? Just when it's you and me of course. I really liked this hydration exercise — hope you did — hope you want more. And if you'd like the president's office to hear about our exercise, or Coach Erickson, that can be arranged. But I don't think you want that — do you, Tony?"

Tony shook his head No.

"Good. Neither do I. I like doin' stuff with you, coach. You're a real inspiration," said Diesel as he continued rubbing Tony's hairy ass inside the football pants. "I'd like to be an All State Tight End like you some day. Think I'll ever be as good a tight end as you...Tony" asked Diesel with a grin as he started rubbing his index finger along Tony's asscrack.

Tony was so confused at the moment. He was not only dealing with the fact that he'd just had some wild sex with one of his students, and he really liked it, but he was now thinking about what trouble he'd be in if anyone found out. He feared that Diesel's version would be accepted more than the truth. And, he kept coming back to the fact that he had liked what just happened.

"Let's see what I need to shoot for," said Diesel as be forced Tony backwards and onto the desk. He yanked off Tony's pants, "You won't need these for a while." Tony's fat cock rested on his abs.

"Diesel, don't, please...let's..." said Tony, now completely naked, laying on his back on the desk with Diesel hovering over him. He knew he could overpower the kid, but that could lead to a fight, with bruises and blood, and who'd be believed in the end?

"Let's what, coach, let's what?" asked Diesel and he pressed between Tony's firm pecs with one hand, forcing him to stay flat, and rubbed the fingers of his other hand up and down Tony's sweaty hairy trench stopping to press each digit lightly on the puckered doorway, and glancing at Tony's sagging nuts.

"I say it's time; let's see how tight of a tight end you are." Diesel shoved a finger into Tony's ass. Tony responded with a blood curdling scream.

"Sounds like no one's been in your end zone in a while," said Diesel. He pulled his finger out and shoved it again, harder. Another scream. "Maybe never," whispered Diesel as he pulled out his finger, picked up Coach E's bottle of baby oil and poured some on his rock hard dick.

"Look, Tony, I'm gonna score with this," said Diesel as he looked down and slathered the baby oil on his dick. Tony lifted his head, not able to lift any more of himself with Diesel still pressing forcefully on his chest, and stared wide eyed at the glistening rod.

Before Tony had a chance to react further, Diesel grabbed each Tony's thighs, pulled Tony toward him so that his legs ended up propped against the sides of Diesel's shoulders, and then quickly reached forward between Tony's legs and pinned him to the desk by locking onto each of Tony's muscular shoulders. His angry red dickhead was pressed against Tony's puckered asshole. Tony's cock shrunk a bit.

"Coach, lemme in. You can enjoy this or I can rip you apart. It's your choice. Pretend you're taking a shit. C'mon, it'll make it a lot easier...and believe me, you're gonna love it," Diesel purred as he rhythmically pressed his cockhead against Tony's wet hairy asshole.

Tony thought quickly that if he pretended to give in, he could catch Diesel at a weak point and turn the tables. He just wanted this whole horrible thing to end. He pressed down as if he was shitting.

"Aaaiiiiiggggghhhhh!" came out of Tony's mouth at a pitch higher than he'd ever hit in his life. Diesel had felt the slight relaxation of Tony's asshole and shoved forward as hard as he could getting half his dick inside Tony's shit chute.

"Easy, coach, easy. Lay still," said Diesel as he massaged Tony's shoulders. Tony's plan went completely out of his head as he experienced the pain of Diesel's telephone pole shooting into his ass. He couldn't remember ever feeling that much pain at one time. And Diesel was overcome with that almost drugged feeling of how good it felt to have his cock inside the warm furnace of an ass. He pulled out slowly, enjoying the excruciating pleasure of Tony's warm insides pressing and shifting for his retreating battering ram. When just his head was still inside, Diesel reversed and pressed forward, groaning with the pleasurable feeling as Tony's insides parted for his rod on its journey inward. He pulled out again, slowly, and pressed in again, slowly. Again. And again. Diesel sensed Tony's body relaxing slightly. He took a moment to admire the firm torso in front of him. By now, sweat had matted most of Tony's hair to his body. Diesel could easily make out the ridges of coach's six pack, and his smooth firm pecs, their arcs interrupted only by the hard nipples standing at attention.

"That's it, coach. See? What did I tell you? Feels good, doesn't it?" asked Diesel quietly and soothingly. Without interrupting his fucking, working to get more of his dick inside Tony's ass with each thrust, he moved one hand to the center of Tony's chest, picked up the bottle of baby oil with the other, and poured some on Tony's crotch. He set the bottle down, moved a hand to each of Tony's pecs and started massaging them. He grunted as he worked Tony's hairy pecs while keeping his eyes on the thick clear oil spreading over Tony's flaccid cock and coating his pubic hair.

Tony jerked and let out a yelp. "Joy button, Tony, I just hit your joy button. Here, I'll do it again," said Diesel as he pumped his hips forward, pulling on Tony's nipples at the same time. Tony yelped again as his breathing began to deepen. Tony no longer felt pain, but his ass felt incredibly full — a feeling he'd never had before. Whatever that 'joy button' was, Tony wanted Diesel to hit it again and again.

Diesel was pretty sure that Tony had given himself over to the fuck and moved one of his hands to Tony's crotch. He started to massage Tony's relaxed shaft. He let out a groan as he noticed that some of the oil he'd poured onto Tony had run down over his ballsack and had now reached Diesel's dick as it moved more quickly in and out of Tony's oven, adding more lubrication to the works. Tony's dick started to respond to the muscleboy's hand working it. Diesel sensed his coming climax. Though he tried to slow his thrusts to extend the pleasure, his need to nut was greater. He let go of Tony's dick, grabbed either side of Tony's waist and fucked senselessly in and out of the warm tunnel of flesh. At the last minute, he pulled out, grabbed his steel hard cock with both hands and began pumping it.

All Tony realized that the thing giving him great pleasure in his ass was suddenly gone. In his sexual stupor he raised himself up on his elbows, asking, "Diesel?"

Diesel grunted with each spurt of cum racing out of his dick. He jetted lines of hot cum all over Tony's stomach, chest, and neck. He even landed a glob on one of Tony's cheeks. As his dick reached the point where the cum came out of his slit like a slow faucet, Diesel fell forward and mashed his mouth against Tony's as they kissed passionately.

Lips still locked, Diesel lifted Tony off the desk and moved him to the floor. Their bodies were in full contact. Diesel slid his hard muscled body on top of Tony's, focusing on their crotches. Tony's arms were wrapped around Diesel, roaming his smooth muscled back. Diesel broke the kiss and held his head a few inches above Tony's. As he spoke, sweat dripped from his face onto Tony's.

"So, how was it, coach? How did you like having a fat hot dick up your ass? Did you like those fireworks?" Tony responded by lifting his head with an open mouth. Diesel met his begging lips with the force of his own, raping Tony's mouth with his tongue. Diesel kept up the sliding motion on top of Tony, staying hard because of the sensual feeling of all that cum coated hair rubbing against his smooth skin. Diesel felt Tony hardening quickly. Diesel broke the kiss again, slid a hand between their bodies, and grabbed Tony's dick.

"Turnaround is fair play, huh, coach? How 'bout I give up my ass to your Italian sausage? You ready for the fuck of your life?" Diesel asked as he raised himself, breaking the cum seal between them to bring himself to a seated position facing Tony. Diesel slid his ass back and forth along Tony's dick, trapped between the muscleboy's asscheeks. He was still rock hard.

"Yeah, this big thing was what was giving you pleasure," said Diesel as he grabbed his cock with one hand as Tony's raised head stared. "And now you're gonna do the same for me," continued Diesel as he slid back enough to be able to grab Tony's dark hard sausage. Before reaching for the baby oil, Diesel slid Tony's shoulder pads underneath his head. He wanted to make sure Tony got to see what was happening along with feeling it. Diesel poured baby oil liberally onto Tony's dick while caressing it with his other hand. This whole time, Tony's hands roamed back and forth along what he could reach of Diesel's legs. The sexual workout they had gone through had both men pumped. Tony was now enthralled looking at Diesel's sweaty muscled body. The physical activity now caused veins to pop out all over Diesel's body that Tony's eyes hungrily travelled along.

Diesel set the oil down and got into a crouched position, holding Tony's massive pole aimed upward toward Diesel's approaching muscled ass. Diesel stopped as Tony's piss slit kissed his pucker. Diesel eased his asshole open just enough to let in about half of Tony's flared cockhead, then pulled off. He did it again. Third time, he let the whole head pop in, squeezed, and then pulled off. Tony was breathing heavily and started fucking motions upward, eager to get that feeling on his dick again.

"Slow down, coach. Let me show you how it's done. I know what I'm doin'" said Diesel, staring at Tony, crouched over the heaving Italian stud, rubbing a hand on Tony's chest. "You just keep an eye on your missile, 'K, Tony?" Diesel started sliding Tony's cock into his ass. Tony bent his head backwards, let out a groan, and shoved his pelvis up.

"I told you, let ME do it, Tony!" yelled Diesel as he quickly pulled himself off of Tony's dick, placing his hands behind him, pressing down on Tony's hips to keep him flat on the floor.

"I'm sorry, Diesel. Please...get on me again...please...my dick..." pleaded Tony.

Diesel began his descent once again. Halfway down he stopped and squeezed his ass ring, getting a yelp out of Tony. Tony just stared at his dark vein covered dick, as it disappeared from sight millimeter by agonizing millimeter. He'd fucked plenty of women in his life, but no pussy, EVER felt this good. He sensed an almost constant stream of precum pouring out into Diesel's chute.

"Ready?"

Tony nodded.

Diesel slid all the way home, slamming his smooth ass onto Tony's pubes. As Diesel anticipated, Tony went into overload and pushed up so hard with his pelvis that he lifted all of Diesel's weight almost a foot in the air. For a minute, Diesel felt like he was riding a bull at a rodeo. Diesel also knew he had to squeeze Tony's dick as hard as he could.

When Diesel's hard ass slammed down, Tony's mind went blindingly white and he felt his balls shoot upward and cum moving toward his cock at lightening speed. He thrust upward and began involuntarily pumping his cum. But something happened. Something was putting such force on the base of his dick that his pumps weakened. He lifted his torso, locked eyes with Diesel and realized what was going on.

"We wanna make this last a bit, don't we, Tony?" asked Diesel as he gradually released his ass's vice like grip on Tony's torpedo. Tony groaned and fell back to the floor, his head banging onto the shoulder pads.

"Tony...don't worry...I told you, you're gonna love this. Watch." Diesel started to stand up from his seated position. Tony stared, his mouth slack, spittle in each corner, as he watched his dick appearing magically in front of him. Diesel rose so that only Tony's head was still inside the furnace. Tony stared back and forth between his tower of a dick and Diesel's hardened member pointing upwards from Diesel's crotch. Diesel had been balancing himself with a hand on each of Tony's upraised knees. He grabbed his oiled dick with one hand and started to slowly pump it.

"Yeah, feast your eyes on all this, coach. Your dick locked into my ass and me pumping myself...just for you." Diesel's cock burped out some precum that made a slow stringy descent to Tony's hairy abs. Tony reached forward with one hand and rubbed the precum into his stomach.

Diesel started a very slow descent, still beating his own cock with one hand. A couple of inches before bottoming out, he dropped to Tony's body, causing Tony to grunt. Diesel pressed his own cock forward till it was lying on Tony's stomach and started rubbing it back a forth sideways along Tony's abs. Tony grabbed Diesel's cock with both hands, took it away from Diesel, and started pumping it.

"Fuck! I've never felt anything like this in my life!" bellowed Tony as he stared at the huge slippery cock in his hands. He pumped a shot of precum into Diesel's scalding insides. Diesel responded with a squeeze. Diesel leaned forward placing a hand on the floor on either side of the prone Italian bringing his face close to Tony's.

"Let's say we go for the extra point, huh, coach?" Tony had locked eyes with Diesel and just nodded in response. Diesel pushed himself up slightly and started fucking himself on Tony's dick. He'd squeeze his ass ring on each journey down, pull up, and then begin again. Tony had let go of Diesel's dick and his hands were now roaming over the hairless hard torso hovering above him. Diesel started moving faster. Tony's entire body began quivering each time Diesel went on his upward journey. As he moved faster, Diesel moved his hands to Tony's chest, landing on his pecs, each hand grabbing a handful of hairy flesh to hold on to.

Diesel fucked faster. The muscles in his arms bunched as he squeezed Tony's pecs, pulling on the hair there. Tony's eyes rolled back in his head, he let go of Diesel's chest. In unison, Tony's arms and legs went rigid and lifted in the air as he climaxed. He shot load after load after load into Diesel's steamy ass, his arms and legs twitching with each pump. His mouth opened wide in a silent scream, the veins in his neck looking like they were about to pop. He passed out.

Diesel sat on Tony's now relaxed body getting his breathing under control. He started to stand, wobbled, and slid back down onto Tony's still hard dick. He was exhausted. Diesel used his strong arms to drag himself backwards between Tony's outstretched legs, freeing himself from Tony's torpedo with a pop. As he rested a moment, breathing a bit more regularly, he felt the mixture of Tony's cum and his own juices dribbling out of his asshole onto the office floor. He pulled himself up to a standing position, holding on to the desk and stared down at Tony.

"You are one hot fuck, you hairy paisano. And you're not an All State Tight End. Buddy, you are one All Fuckin' American Tight End!" Diesel picked up the towel Tony had pulled off of him, wrapped it around his neck, and headed for the office shower. As he grabbed the handle, he turned back to Tony and said to the drowsy coach,

"Hey, Tony, join me if you want. I promise to drop the soap at least once."

CHAPTER 6

The School Therapist

"OK, Diesel, obviously our talks are not helping," fumed Greg Thompson, the school therapist, as he paced back and forth in his office. He was really getting tired of this cocky jerk. Diesel slouched in the office chair, legs spread wide, basket bulging, a smirk on his face with his hands locked behind his head, his massive arms cocked up and on display.

He'd been fighting again. Something that was supposed to have stopped by having regular meetings with Dr. Thompson. Diesel enjoyed the sessions, not only because Dr. Thompson was a friendly ear, but also because he so enjoyed teasing Dr. Thompson with his muscle bound body. He knew Thompson wanted him, but then again, who didn't? But he knew he was in danger once again of becoming ineligible for sports because of his fighting, and at the moment, playing in sports was the only interesting thing about college for Diesel.

"I'm going to try hypnosis. It's a desperate move, but nothing else seems to work. I don't want to see you get into more trouble. Are you OK with that?" asked Greg standing next to his desk looking down at the seated stud, forcing himself to limit his lust for the guy to raping him with his eyes. He'd only met with Diesel six times so far but he'd already gotten to the point where he fantasized about Diesel all the time. When he wasn't fantasizing about Diesel, he was thinking about how arrogant he was.

At his second session, a pair of dirty socks fell out of the gym bag that Diesel had with him all the time. Greg grabbed them when Diesel wasn't looking. He would masturbate while smelling the socks. For the last week Greg had been beating off into them and they were now pretty rank and crusty.

Greg wasn't dumb. And he figured Diesel wasn't either. Each knew what was going on but they just didn't say anything out loud. Diesel would come to the sessions "dressed for sex" — as Greg saw it — tight clothes, or baggy jeans that seemed to be held up only by the combined bulges of his hard bubblebutt and gigantic dick, shirts that only emphasized his enormous chest, rock hard arms, and bulging abs. Sometimes, pretending he was distracted by some thought, Diesel would bounce his slabs of pecmeat which would always get Greg instantly hard. He'd also use the excuse of needing a break to do some slow stretches in front of Greg, his muscles shifting and rolling all over his body as Greg would ineffectively try not to drink in the sight.

"You mean where you do things like make me dance like a chicken?"

"Cut the crap, Diesel, I'm serious. People are susceptible to hypnosis to different degrees. And all it is is a tool to help people either start or stop doing things. There are things called post-hypnotic suggestions — the chicken dance thing — but those are party tricks and I'm talking some serious work here. How 'bout it? Can we try it?"

Diesel flexed his biceps a few times while Dr. Thompson spoke. "Sure," said Diesel. "Could be fun," he thought.

Greg was surprised at how quickly Diesel went under. One advantage was that Greg could now stare at the kid as much as he wanted — and stare he did. "Fuck, the kid has muscles on his muscles! And I don't know how he is able to walk straight with that monster hanging between his legs," thought Greg. Diesel sat up in the chair, hunched slightly forward, eyes closed, breathing slowly and deeply, his meaty arms hanging at his sides.

Today he was wearing a v-neck white sweater...tight...real tight. Not only could Greg see Diesel's pert nipples, but he gazed at Diesel's pecs as they almost imperceptibly rhythmically swayed with his breathing, looking like they were ready to burst the material of the sweater.

Greg didn't have much experience with hypnotism but he'd studied it some in med school and had read some journal articles on it. He asked Diesel a set of questions to determine his truth telling state — name, age, etc. He said his favorite sport was wrestling and least favorite was swimming. Greg asked him why swimming was his least favorite.

"I don't like it because it's not a contact sport. It's me against others, but not one on one. Besides, I'm not built for swimming...too bulky." Greg imagined Diesel in a pair of Speedos and thought, "Guy, you are built for everything!" Part of what he wanted to accomplish with the hypnotism sessions was to have Diesel focus on positive aspects of things so he asked Diesel to tell him even though it was his least favorite sport, what positive things could be associate with it.

"Money."

"How is money related to your swimming, Diesel?"

"Mr. Peters pays me for letting him take pictures and videos of me at practice and in his studio. He also pays for sex."

"Well, this is certainly an interesting turn of events," thought Greg. "Why does he take pictures of you?" he asked.

"He's retired with lots of money and really into all the digital video stuff. He's trying to make a video of me fucking around with myself."

"I don't understand, Diesel, explain it to me."

"Mr. Peters thinks I'm really hot and he wants to make a film for himself of me doing stuff with myself, like kissing, touching, rubbing, and all that. He's already been able to edit some stuff where he's got me giving another me a blow job. Right now he's working on one where I'd fuck myself."

Greg's mouth was open in shock. "How do you give yourself a blow job?"

"I don't know how he does it but it's pretty freaky to see. He's filmed me while I hold my mouth as wide open as I can and he's filmed my dick when it's hard. Somehow he's able to put everything together so there are two of me on the screen at the same time, one getting a blow job and the other doing the sucking. It looks real...kinda hot, but freaky."

"You said he films you at practice...how?"

"You know how we have the two pools next to each other here? When meets are going on, coach encourages those of us not in the meets to practice in the other pool, kind of a show of support for the ones who are competing. Mr. Peters is in the stands and films me while I practice. He pays me pretty well for it. He has me wear blue Speedos with the lining cut out. When I'm not doing laps, I'm out of the water hitting different poses that he gets on film. He likes it when I'm pretty wet, says it looks good on film and with the blue suit all wet he says it's easier to remove it through editing."

"When's your next practice?"

"Tomorrow afternoon."

Greg spent the rest of the session taking Diesel through some positive imagery work and before he brought Diesel out of his trance, he told him that he wouldn't remember anything about the swimming part of their discussion.

Greg really wanted to touch Diesel. He wanted to feel what he imagined to be hot firm mounds of flesh. But decided against it. He did plant the post hypnotic suggestion that Diesel would feel that both his nipples were itching once he came out of the trance, and that the need to scratch them would go away once he left Dr. Thompson's office.

"OK, Diesel, how do you think the first session went?" asked Greg.

"I guess OK," said Diesel somewhat tentatively.

Dr. Thompson and Diesel spent the next fifteen minutes talking about the goals of the hypnotism sessions. Greg was amused and aroused by how Diesel would frequently rub at one nipple, slowly, then the other. He acted like he didn't even notice he was doing it. Greg actually ended the meeting early when it reached the point where merely rubbing the nubs was not enough and Diesel began alternately pinching each nipple through the sweater, again, seeming to not even notice what he was doing. Greg could see Diesel's tense face relax and his eyes go unfocused momentarily each time he'd give a nipple a really good squeeze. Greg didn't want his rising sexual fever to take over so he ended the session.

The next afternoon Greg couldn't keep himself from stopping by the school swimming pools. Sports are big all over Texas, and it was no different here. Having two pools seemed more like the rule than the exception. Greg sat at the far end of the pools, on the side by the practice pool. He spotted the infamous Mr. Peters in the stands on the opposite side with a camera on a tripod. Greg knew it was focused on Diesel though you couldn't tell that from just looking.

And then he spotted Diesel. Even from this distance, the sight took Greg's breath away. He was one of three guys practicing. The bulk of everyone's attention was directed to the competition going on in the other pool, but the bulk named Diesel held the attention of Greg and Mr. Peters, and probably a few others in the stands Greg was not aware of. Greg wouldn't have been at all surprised to discover that Diesel might have a fan club enthralled with this blond studpuppy.

The other two guys practicing in the pool with Diesel, though built for swimming, looked almost anorexic next to the hulking mass of Diesel. Even from a distance, Greg could see some of Diesel's body parts in motion. He could see Diesel facing toward Mr. Peters' camera, bouncing his pecs. More than once he'd put his back to the camera, and under the guise of drying off the front of his body, he would rhythmically tense and relax his glutes for the camera. At one point, he laid down on the diving board and "exercised" by lifting his arms and legs, touching each other while they were pointed upward. Greg visualized ravaging Diesel's asshole while Diesel's legs tensed upward in the air. When he then stood up on the diving board preparing to dive into the water, his Speedos had ridden up a bit in the back and both asscheeks were peeking out a bit.

A few times, while still in the water, Diesel would shoot up, grab the diving board from underneath and do pull-ups on it. Greg could actually see Diesel's gigantic coiled dick bounce underneath the almost transparent blue Speedo each time he jutted out of the water. He'd hold himself at the top of the pull-up for a teasing moment... so many muscles tensed with his monster of a dick bouncing as if in slow motion, water cascading over the musclegod's ripped mass. Greg realized his own dick was hurting in its hardness, and left the pool area, covering his bulge with a jacket, afraid that his leaking precum would seep through the pants material at any moment.

At their next session, after putting Diesel under, Greg asked him to tell him more about what happens with Mr. Peters.

"Well, he buys me a lot of clothes and likes to take me out to dinner. He's not a bad guy but he is sure nuts about my body." Today, Diesel was wearing nylon gym shorts, and a wife beater covered by a short sleeved form fitting button down shirt. Only the bottom couple of buttons were buttoned. The top shirt flared open from Diesel's waist toward his shoulders showcasing his bulging chest.

"Did he buy you what you're wearing today?"

"No. He buys me mainly real expensive stuff or real sexy stuff."

"You don't think you're dressed sexy right now?"

"Oh, no, I do think I'm dressed sexy. The sexy stuff Mr. Peters buys me is like underwear stuff and leather and latex and stuff like that."

"Why do you dress sexy, Diesel?"

"Cause I know it helps me get whatever I want. I know I've got a great body and I like to show it off and I like it when people show appreciation for my body."

"Do you like to tease people with your body, Diesel?"

"Sure."

"Who do you tease?"

"People like you."

Greg was a bit taken aback by Diesel's answer. But then he realized that Diesel was in a hypnotic trance and was answering things straightforwardly. "How do you mean, 'people like you'"?

"Guys who are hot for me. Guys who I could make them do things. Guys who could do things for me. Guys who would do things for me if I let them fuck around with me."

"What could I do for you, Diesel?"

"You could talk to the coaches and tell them that I'm working on not fighting so much."

"But how could I say those things if they weren't true?"

"If I let you do things to me that I know you want to, you'd do it."

Greg had an idea. "Diesel, stand up." Diesel stood. He was relaxed, arms and head hanging loosely. Greg wanted to see just how far he could take this cocky stud. He was really irritated with how arrogant Diesel was. He had to find some way to knock that out of him. Right now, all he wanted to do was be entertained at Diesel's expense. Ethics were out the window. He just wanted to see this prick looking stupid.

"When I snap my fingers, you're going to take your shirts off, pull your shorts down, sit down in the chair, and play with yourself. You'll keep your eyes open and focused on me. You're going to continue doing that while we keep working, but you're not going to get hard. When I snap my fingers again, you'll stop playing with yourself and get dressed. You'll remain in this hypnotized state the whole time. Do you understand, Diesel?"

"Yes, sir."

Greg snapped his fingers. Diesel lifted his head, opened his eyes, and smiled at Greg. He took his shirts off, pulled his shorts down, sat down in the chair, and started squeezing and tugging on his dick, first with one hand, then both. Every once in a while, the fingertips of one hand would run up and down the center ridge of Diesel's eight pack abs. He never took his eyes from Greg's.

"Tell me more about Mr. Peters. Does he ever touch you?"

"Oh yeah, he touches me. He touches me a lot. He's got a really nice place, like an estate, outside the city where I sometimes stay overnight. There's a full gym there, a swimming pool, and really nice video equipment. He gives amazing massages. He massages me sometimes when I'm standing, but mainly when I'm laying on a table. The massages are incredible. And he's got cameras all over the place filming from different angles. He tells me that he does the massages so that he can understand how big each of my muscles is and how they work together so that when he works on the video of me he can make it more realistic."

By this time, Greg didn't care that his goal of humiliating Diesel fell by the wayside. He was incredibly aroused at the sight of Diesel sitting in front of him, almost completely naked, yanking on his huge penis, rubbing his chest and staring at him. Greg couldn't resist. With a groan he pulled out his own dick, proudly hardened to just over seven inches, and started pumping it. Diesel's eyes never strayed from looking into Greg's. Greg's eyes roamed all over Diesel's seated body, ending up staring back into the stud's eyes.

"One thing I don't like though is that what he likes to do is first get me all relaxed laying on my back and then massage me and get me excited to the point where I'm about to blow my load, and cuts me off. It kinda makes me shake all over. It's like I got a rocket inside my body shooting really fast all over the place trying to bust out and it can't get out. I almost see stars. Mr. Peters says that when this happens it makes my face look real real sexy and that it will help him with the video. The most I let him do it is three times because by then I really gotta get off. He slides one of my legs off the table and starts humping against it till he cums. At the same time he's jerkin' the hog here till I pop a load."

Greg went rigid while Diesel was talking about how Mr. Peters said Diesel's face looked really sexy, slipped to the edge of his chair, started jerking and sent spurt after spurt of his thick hot cum toward Diesel. Greg recovered from his climax after Diesel stopped talking. He looked horrified as he noticed sprays of his cum on Diesel.

"Diesel, I want you to stand up now so I can wipe something off your skin. Is that OK with you?"

"Sure," said Diesel as he stood, still pulling at his flaccid yet massive cock with one hand, while the other rubbed up and down his torso, spreading around Greg's load absentmindedly.

"Diesel, stop rubbing yourself. Let that hand fall to your side." Diesel complied. Greg pulled a small towel out from one of his desk drawers and began wiping Diesel's torso, removing his own cum mixed with a light layer of Diesel's sweat. This was the first time Greg had actually touched Diesel and he loved the feel of the hard muscles covered with a silky layer of skin. Diesel continued to attempt to keep in eye contact with Greg. Satisfied that he had removed everything, Greg looked at Diesel's face and only then noticed a shot of cum just below Diesel's lower lip. He trembled.

"Diesel, I'm going to have to use my mouth to clean one area on your face, OK?"

"Sure, that's fine, Dr. Thompson."

Greg grabbed onto each of Diesel's firm arms and pulled himself to Diesel. His dick was still rock hard, standing straight up still dripping some cum. He pressed his crotch into Diesel's feeling Diesel's arm as it continued to tug on the hog. Greg tilted his head sideways opening his mouth moving closer to Diesel's. He stopped just short of touching lips, letting Diesel's hot breath hit him like a soft pillow tapping. He locked onto Diesel's lower lip with his lips, sucking and moaning, running his wet tongue on Diesel's lip and chin. He could feel the heat of Diesel's torso through his shirt. Finally, he pulled away and shakily sat back down in his chair.

"OK, Diesel, remember this time when I snap my fingers I want you to stop playing with yourself and get dressed. When you're done getting dressed, sit down in the chair and wait for more instructions. You'll remain in this hypnotic state." Diesel dressed himself quietly and sat down.

"Diesel, you know that we are working to deal with your aggression, aren't we?"

"Yes, doctor, we are."

"I think that one thing that might help is if you try and make amends with someone you've been aggressive to in the past. Is there someone here at school you've been mean to or taken advantage of recently?"

"Yes."

"Who, Diesel."

"There have actually been a lot of them."

"Well, let's take it step by step. Who's the first one that comes to mind?"

"Danny. He's on the wrestling team with me."

"Were you mean to him?"

"Not exactly."

"Then what?"

"I guess I took advantage of him."

"How?"

"He's also a senior, on the wrestling team with me, and I knew he really had the hots for me...bad. I'm not usually interested in guys unless they're pretty built or older and more assertive. Danny's a small guy, about 5'7", but I really liked the looks of Danny's butt and ended up throwing him a really powerful fuck and I shouldn't have done it since I was just taking advantage of the fact that he wanted me bad."

"How do you think you could make this up to him, Diesel?"

"I could apologize."

"Yes, you should apologize. You should explain to him why you did what you did, that you're sorry for it, and you want to make it up to him. Find out what you can do to make it up to him and do that. Whatever he wants is what you'll do. Once that's done, you'll feel better and maybe you won't be as inclined to take advantage of people in the future."

"OK, Dr. Thompson, I'll do that."

Greg then talked more with Diesel about recognizing behavioral patterns that might lead to Diesel's becoming aggressive, and ways to avoid those routes. Before Greg brought him out of his hypnotic state, he instructed Diesel to not remember anything about what they had covered that day, or anything that had happened, except their discussion on aggressive patterns, and that he would still want to make amends with the Danny kid as they had discussed, though he wouldn't remember the discussion they'd just had leading up to Diesel's decision to apologize.

"So how do you think your hypnotism therapy is going, Diesel?"

"I guess it's going OK. We spent the whole time talking about what makes me get angry and that was pretty interesting. I also feel really relaxed after each session. Guess that means they're good for me. Thanks for not giving up on me, Dr. Thompson," said Diesel as he stood to leave and shook Greg's hand. The courteous move caught Greg a bit off guard. That, in addition to the fact that while their hands were clasped, Diesel was looking at Greg the same way he had just been looking at him when he was hypnotized, and Greg could only think about how he was holding the hand that just a short time ago was rubbing Greg's cum all over his young muscled torso.

The next session was almost two weeks later due to both of their schedules. Dr. Thompson was gone for a few days at a conference in Seattle and Diesel had two swimming meets and a wrestling meet a few of days apart from each other and begged off making an appointment till after the meets. He showed up at Dr. Thompson's office in a particularly jocular mood as he had done better than he had hoped to do at both swim meets and once again took top honors in wrestling, as he usually did.

He was also looking forward to a few days in a row of time he'd have to use as he wished. He could think of a number of ways he could make some quick money using his body, and he knew he was looking particularly good at the moment following his recent heavy workouts in preparation for the meets. Besides, he hadn't had a chance to tease Dr. Thompson in two whole weeks!

Little did he know that Greg had gotten back from his conference just in time to make it to Diesel's wrestling meet at UT Austin. Greg added a whole new vein of Diesel fantasies after watching Diesel's body, barely contained in a wrestling singlet, manhandling one opponent after another. Greg especially loved the hungry look he saw in Diesel's eyes any time he and his opponent were on their feet pacing around each other. Greg was impressed how focused Diesel was during his matches — nothing existed for Diesel except getting his opponent to submit.

"You look like things are going well for you. Diesel," said Greg while they shook hands. Each took their respective seats. Diesel was wearing a faded red t-shirt, too small of course, white baggy nylon gym shorts with black stretch shorts underneath, and a pair of black lace up boots that looked very similar to wrestling boots.

"You could say that. Hey, Dr. Thompson, I want to thank you again for letting me go two weeks between sessions. I did great in my swim and wrestling meets, and I didn't get in a single fight the whole time!" he said with a white toothy grin. He sat in the chair, a hand resting on either knee, giving the impression that he was ready to leap out of the chair at any moment. For the first time, Greg noticed what a contrast there was between Diesel's muscular masculine body and the yellow blonde curly hair on his head that looked almost too soft to touch. He imagined his fists entangled in the golden locks while he would be jerking Diesel's head back and forth raping the muscleboy's mouth with his dick.

"Ready to go under, Diesel?"

"Give it your best shot, Doc!"

The first thing Greg had Diesel do once in a hypnotic state was remove his clothing, keeping the boots on. He also instructed Diesel that at some point he might again be touched and if so, to let it happen. Greg had missed seeing this stud's body in the flesh.

While going through the usual exercises on aggressive thoughts and deeds, Greg had Diesel walking around the office. He loved seeing Diesel's body from different angles, and really liked watching the manboy's muscle's ripple in different places as he moved and was particularly aroused by the fact that the black boots remained on.

At one point, he had Diesel press up against a wall standing spread-eagled with arms spread out above him and pretending to be fucking the wall slowly. Diesel's shoulders looked like they were many times wider than his waist. Greg also liked watching how the sides of Diesel's protruding ass would dimple deeply inward each time he'd push his pelvis slowly into the wall. Finally he had Diesel sit again as he was close to blowing his load, wanted to calm down a bit, and needed to hear about what might have happened with Danny.

"Diesel, did you do anything about what we talked about last time to make things up with Danny?"

"Yes, I did."

"What did you do?"

"I ended up talking to Danny twice but it looked like he didn't believe me either time that I was sorry for what I had done. So then I sent him a text message asking him to forgive me and telling him that I'd do anything he wanted me to do to prove I was telling the truth and was sorry for what I had done to him."

"Then what happened?"

"I didn't think my apology worked until three days ago. It was Saturday late morning; I was at home putting myself through one last intensive workout before my wrestling meet later that day. I was towards the end of the workout, feeling really pumped and tired, but a good tired...sweat was pouring off me. Sitting on my weight bench in the middle of a set of curls, I was actually slipping a bit on the plastic seat since all I had on was a jock, and I was so sweaty. Then I spotted Danny in one of the mirrors, dropped the dumbbell and jumped up."

(Author's Note: This next part of the story is told from Dr. Thompson's point of view — how his mind envisioned the story as Diesel, wearing just a pair of laced up boots, sat in the chair in Greg's office, facing Greg, telling it to him. Greg adds a few details to complete the visual story running in his head.)

"Danny, I'm so glad to see you," said Diesel as he ran to Danny and wrapped him in a bearhug. Danny's face was pressed up against one of Diesel's sweaty pecs and he drank in the dank smell of Diesel's heated flesh. Diesel pulled away, held the smaller guy by his shoulders and said, "Will you please believe me that I am sorry for what I did to you? I will do anything you want...just forgive me... please?" Danny stared into Diesel's pleading eyes, watching sweat run down the musclegod's body in his peripheral vision.

"Diesel, the reason I couldn't talk to you was because I really liked what you did to me. You paid attention to me and you made me feel things in my body that I've never felt before. I want to feel those things again...with you," said Danny as he leaned forward with his mouth open, aiming for Diesel's lips.

Diesel let go of Danny's shoulders with a shove and turned his back to Danny. "No, its wrong, Danny. I shouldn't have done what I did. All I thought about was what I wanted to do to get off. It was wrong. I just wanted to get to that butt of yours; I was only thinking of myself."

Danny stared at Diesel's muscled back, the bumps of hard muscles shining in the sunlight streaming in through the glass block basement windows, sweat racing down to be sucked into the already sopping waistband of the jockstrap.

"Then if you really want to do the right thing, you'll do what I want to do, and think about what I want to do to get off...this time...not what you want. You said you'd do anything I wanted you to do to prove you were telling the truth," said Danny as his hands started lightly rubbing Diesel's back. "God, Diesel, you are so fucking hot, and I want you to make me feel the way I felt the last time we were together here in your gym," said Danny as his hands dropped to Diesel's ass, one hand squeezing one of the hard wet asscheeks, the other moving slowly up and down Diesel's asscrack.

Diesel turned around to face Danny. "I'll do whatever you want, little buddy. I'm yours," said Diesel as he pulled off his jockstrap and threw it across the room. He stood in front of Danny, covered in sweat, as his telephone pole of a dick swayed back and forth.

Danny ripped off the t-shirt, shorts and sandals he was wearing, grabbed the swaying baseball bat of a dick and locked his mouth on one of Diesel's jutting nipples. "God, I love your chest, Diesel," he mumbled while spit ran freely from his mouth all over Diesel's chest.

"Make them hard for me, Diesel, hard!" begged Danny as he pulled away and stared at Diesel's chest. Diesel tensed his pecs and they became rock hard in an instant. All he wanted to do now was please this kid. Danny let go of Diesel's dick and let his hands roam over the twin mounds of hardened flesh, lubricated by the layer of sweat on Diesel's skin. Danny slapped one of the pecs, then the other. Then he slapped them a few times in unison, loving the sharp sound made when his hand met the muscled flesh. He formed fists with his hands and began punching the steel hard slabs. He hit them harder and harder, now loving the deep thumping noise that made.

"Oh, yeah, little buddy, punch those suckers!" moaned Diesel, half in sensual pleasure, half in desire to please Danny. Danny's fists became a blur and suddenly Diesel relaxed the muscles. Danny squealed in pleasure as his fists suddenly switched from hitting a wall to hitting what felt like soft hot tar.

"Lay down!" Danny ordered. Diesel fell down on his back, legs and arms spread wide. Danny fell on his musclegod's body and locked lips with him, sucking hungrily while grinding his dick into Diesel's lumpy abs.

"I wanna fuck you, Diesel...bad!"

Diesel broke the kiss, "Whatever you want, Danny, my ass is yours!"

Danny laughed. "My dick would get lost in your ass...I want to try something different," said Danny as he slid up a bit on Diesel's hard muscled body. Danny's hardened dick stood up, his balls resting between Diesel's pecs.

"I wanna fuck you here. Press your pecs together," ordered Danny as he pushed his hard cock down into the sweaty valley between Diesel's pecs.

"Your wish is my command, sir," said Diesel as each of his meaty hands grabbed the outside of one of his pecs and pressed them together surrounding Danny's cock like a lava flow. Danny's eyes popped open as he felt his dick being surrounded by Diesel's hot flesh. He started to pump back and forth inside the heated mass of chest flesh.

Diesel stared up at Danny's face and saw his eyes closed tightly, mouth slightly ajar with a bit of spittle in the corner of his mouth. All Diesel wanted was to make sure Danny was feeling good. And it looked like that was the case considering the gradual increase in the speed at which Danny fucked against Diesel's chest.

"Ohhhhhhh....Dieeeeeeeesel...ohhhhhhhhhhhhhh," Danny kept moaning over and over as he fucked between the mashed mountains of pec muscle. Danny's arms were on the floor outside of Diesel's shoulders. As he approached climax, his arm muscles gave way and he fell downward on top of Diesel, his chest on Diesel's face. On autopilot, he kept fucking. Diesel opened his mouth and began giving Danny's chest wet kisses.

Danny screamed as he unloaded his cream onto Diesel's chest, overcome by the pleasure of the strong pulses of cum combined with Diesel's tongue work on his own chest. Spiraling back down to earth, Danny propped himself up and gave Diesel a long wet kiss. Their tongues battled as they moaned into each other's mouths.

Scooting down on Diesel's hard body, Danny fell in between Diesel's outstretched massive legs, his hands grabbing Diesel's flaccid cock. He began licking the monster. Then he attached his mouth to it, sucking as hard as he could. As Danny's mouth moved up and down the length of the tube of dickflesh, he actually started gnawing on the spongy flesh. Diesel felt the sting of Danny's teeth on his cock but was determined to let Danny have his way. Danny started chewing on the stalk like it was a freshly roasted ear of corn dripping with hot butter.

Diesel was not initially enjoying his fellow wrestler's teeth biting into his sperm shooter. Danny's hands released their hold on the stalk and started rubbing Diesel's ab muscles. The massage did the trick for turning the pain of the chewing teeth on his dick into a twisted pleasure; Diesel's dick started to harden. Danny felt the hardening and chewed on the stalk even more, moaning into the cockflesh in a frenzy of desire. Danny began biting the hard cock in earnest. Diesel felt the combination of the excitement and pain, choosing to focus on the excitement in order to allow Danny to have his pleasure.

Danny finally stopped chewing and moved his mouth to Diesel's piss slit as his hands moved back to the steel hard cock, pumping it up and down. Danny sucked on the head and attempted to force his tongue into the piss slit, his teeth locking his mouth onto the hard wet dickhead. Diesel moaned louder and louder as he reached the point of no return. Lying on his back, Diesel's chest pumped in and out, sucking in and blowing out more and more air. His hands grabbed at Danny's head, gently holding it in place, attached to Diesel's gigantic dickhead, which was almost spewing precum.

The first shot of Diesel's cum was so powerful that it made Danny jerk his mouth off the dickhead and out of the grasp of Diesel's hands. Cum continued to spray out of Diesel's cock in long and powerful spurts onto Danny's face and into his hair.

When Diesel's spray was down to a dribble, Danny crawled up Diesel's body. His face was pretty much covered with Diesel's hot white cream. Their lips met in a passionate kiss.

When Danny lifted up, Diesel ran his hands over Danny's face, collected the warm sticky cum, and rubbing it into Danny's scalp. Danny's spiked blonde hair was long enough that the cum plastered his hair to his head.

Diesel began licking Danny's skull, like a mother cat with a new litter. His mouth filled with bits of his own cum, Diesel again locked lips with Danny, spreading the cum around Danny's mouth with his talented tongue.

"I want to keep doing stuff like this with you, Diesel, OK?"

"No problem, kiddo, no problem," said Diesel, panting with Danny's hot body pressed on top of him. Danny reached behind him and took hold of Diesel's spent dick, wet and sticky with cum. He sat up on Diesel's torso and while holding the dick flat against the center ridge of his clearly defined abs, slid back till his ass rested on the sleeping monster of a dick.

"I want you to have my butt again, Diesel," said Danny as he began to slowly slide his asscrack along the length of Diesel's cock, trapped between the twink's asscheeks.

"You like, Mr. Muscles?" Danny asked Diesel with a smile as he scooted back and forth, feeling the monster begin to waken. Diesel was still flat on his back, amazed that this guy wanted to keep going. He could see Danny's adorable bubblebutt in his head as his brain dealt with the almost electric current running from his dick to his brain because that beautiful butt was pressed against his hog, sliding back and forth. With a loud moan, he threw his arms out on either side of him, brought his legs up so his feet were flat on the floor and spread his legs out even further.

"Help me," said Danny as his reached forward toward Diesel. Diesel's massive paws each grabbed one of Danny's forearms and began pushing and pulling the smaller wrestler along his hardening shaft. This went on for about ten minutes, each of them taking turns deciding when to speed up or when to slow down. Diesel's dick finally reached its hardest stage. Danny was amazed feeling the lumpy log running along his trench, remembering that at one time the whole monster was inside him. When he let go of Diesel's arms, Diesel let them flop to the ground stretching outward. Danny fell forward, a hand landing on each of Diesel's nipples. He continued to slide back and forth, pulling hard on Diesel's nipples to jerk himself forward, then pressing the pecs hard to push himself back. Diesel gritted his teeth to deal with the painful pulls on his tits. Every once in a while Danny would slide forward enough for his ass to slap into the puddle of Diesel's precum and then drag it back along the shaft as lubricant.

Danny sensed that Diesel was getting close, watching the blonde god suck air in and out of his lungs. He let go of Diesel's chest, leaned back and wrapped an arm around each of Diesel's upper legs with his hands curving around to rest on Diesel's knees. He wanted to strap himself in for what he felt might be a bumpy ride.

Diesel's head rolled back and forth. He was in a state of ecstasy he rarely reached and didn't notice that Danny had stopped his sliding back and forth. Danny was now just holding on to Diesel's legs while clenching his ass over and over, on Diesel's rock hard dick.

"C'mon, Diesel, shoot for me. Shoot for your Danny. I wanna feel your cum run along my sweet little ass while it races the length of your dick on its way out. I want you to spray a load like you've never sprayed before. My ass wants it, Diesel. I wanna see your cum shoot out over your head. Do it, mother fucker, do it!" yelled Danny as he squeezed his ass muscles over and over as his clenching bubblebutt sucked along the length of Diesel's torpedo of a dick.

Diesel lifted his hips in the air, bellowed, and released the clamp on his firehose. Cum gushed out of his piss slit. The first volley met Danny's desires, flying inches over Diesel's face, landing with a loud splat two feet in front of their bodies. The rest of the load landed on Diesel's face and chest. Danny had tightened his grip on Diesel's legs and watched the streams of white goo shoot out like cannon fire then gradually change to champagne bubbling out of a freshly opened bottle. He fell forward and locked lips with the panting blonde lying on his back.

"Time to get ready for your wrestling meet, Diesel," whispered Danny as his tongue roamed Diesel's face and neck, sucking up the bigger wrestler's freshly spewed load, "I'll be suited up on the bench and I want you to think of me while you're wrestling. My dick will be hard and my ass will be aching for your dick. You win your matches and this ass will be yours to plow!" said Danny as he guided one of Diesel's hands to his warm wet bubblebutt.

(Back to the reality of Dr. Thompson's office.)

Greg sat is his chair, completely dumbfounded, his dick aching, and his underwear damp with precum. It took all his strength to not rape the naked blonde sitting calmly in front of him.

"Was happened at the wrestling meet?"

"All I wanted to do was beat every guy into submission so that I could put my dick back in Danny's butt."

"And did that happen?"

"Yes, doctor. Saturday night Danny let me fuck him while I held him against the wall of my basement. He wanted me to be rougher than I had been before. I only did it because he wanted it, doctor. I really slammed into his ass with my dick, and really slammed him into the wall at the same time. At one point I stopped to see if he was OK."

"And was he?"

"Yes, he was. He actually was a little mad at me for stopping so I got back to fucking him really hard. After I came, he made me stay in him and lay down on my back on the floor. Then he just stayed on top of me using his legs and arms to pump himself slowly back and forth on my dick. It felt really good and I was so spent after the meet and the fucking that I fell asleep within a few minutes. When I woke up, Danny was gone but he left me a note saying he completely forgave me and that he wanted to keep getting together."

Greg had already crossed so many professional lines, and he was so hot to have this studmuffin, he threw caution to the wind, "Diesel, I'm going to bring you out of your hypnotic state in a moment. When I do, you're going to remember the aggression exercises we went through. You will not remember removing your clothes, walking around the office or that you told me what happened between you and Danny. Do you understand, Diesel?"

"Yes, doctor."

"OK when I finish giving you the following instructions, I want you to get dressed and sit back down in the chair. When you leave my office at the end of our session today, you're going to go straight home and work out for a couple of hours. You're going to take yourself through a brutal workout so that your muscles are tired, but you're fully pumped...and wanting to have some sex with a guy. You're going to think about wanting to have sex with a guy all while you work out and the need will just get stronger through the workout. At the end of the workout, you're going to get dressed in some clothing that you think I will find sexy and you're going to come to my home because you've realized that I'm the guy you want to have sex with.

You will not dry yourself off or shower after the workout; you'll just put on the sexy clothes and come to my apartment. When you get there, you're going to talk to me about how much I've helped you with our sessions.

Your need to have sex with me will eventually overpower you. You will offer yourself to me and when I turn you down, you'll then beg to have sex with me. You will find me very attractive. We will end up in my bed, you will tie me in the bed, and then you'll do everything I tell you to do. The whole time your focus will be on making things as pleasurable for me as possible. And you'll do all this without remembering that I told you to do this. You'll just know it's the right thing to do. Do you understand, Diesel?"

"Yes, doctor, I do."

"OK, get dressed and then return to the chair." Greg sighed as he watched parts of Diesel's flesh gradualy get covered up by his shorts and t-shirt, but he knew that he'd soon see all that flesh again, and do whatever he wanted with it.

"Diesel, when I clap my hands, you'll wake up refreshed and wanting to talk about how you've spent your time since our last meeting working on lowering your aggressive tendencies." Dr. Thompson clapped his hands.

Three hours later, Greg was nervously pacing in his apartment clad only in an old pullover shirt and cotton shorts. Then the knock on his door came. Greg grabbed the doorkrob and pulled open the door. It was Diesel of course. Greg could tell by Diesel's sweaty face and matted golden hair that he'd had the workout and had come over straight from it. But he was very disappointed to see Diesel clothed in some old baggy dark blue sweat pants and a long sleeve, matching sweatshirt. On his feet were a pair of bright red leather wrestling boots that looked oddly classy next to the bulky blue cotton.

"Hi, Dr. Thompson, I hope you don't mind my stopping by. I was out for a run and saw your lights on...can I come in, please?"

"Sure, Diesel, sure. Sorry, you caught me by surprise, c'mon in," said Greg as he stepped aside to let the hulking mass walk by him. Even the baggy blue material couldn't hide the fact that Diesel had a massive and firm ass.

Diesel walked in to Greg's living room and then turned to face him, "Dr. Thompson, I just wanted to tell you that I really appreciate all the help you're giving me. Not just with helping me stay away from fighting, but I think whatever else we do...I mean talk about... when I'm hypnotized is also helping me study better and do better in sports." Diesel took a couple of hesitant steps toward Greg, nervously lifted up his arms, then just quickly wrapped Greg in a hug saying, "Doc, you're the greatest!"

Greg could feel Diesel's body pressing against him just about everywhere. His senses starting going into overload as he realized he could feel the lumps of Diesel's abs press against his own firm stomach — pressing back and forth as the musclestud breathed. Greg also felt Diesel's cock on his own thigh. Finally, he broke the embrace.

"Well, thank you, Diesel...thank you very much. I'm not sure what to say. But you know, you're the real reason anything good is happening to you. All I do is try and work with the good that is inside you...bring it out so that you see it there too." Greg was seriously on his way toward popping major bone. He couldn't seem to break eye contact with Diesel, who was looking at Greg with a sad puppy dog look. Greg quickly sat down in a chair.

Diesel walked over to where Greg was seated and squatted down, between Greg's spread legs, putting a hand on the top of each of Greg's thighs. "I really do want to thank you, Doc. You're a really terrific guy. I like you...a lot," Diesel squeezed Greg's thighs with his last two words.

"I like you too, Diesel. You've come a long way in our sessions," said Greg, now unable to stop the rush of blood to his dick. The two guys stared at each other silently for a moment, Diesel caressing Greg's thighs while Greg's dick tented the baggy gym shorts at an obscenely obvious angle.

Not wanting the moment to end, dying to jump Diesel, Greg forced himself to follow his own script. He pushed Diesel's hands off his thighs, "Diesel, I really think you should leave...now. We shouldn't be doing any of this."

Diesel stood, his eyes filling with tears, "OK...I hope I didn't offend you...please don't hate me."

Without even thinking, Greg jumped up and put his arms around Diesel, "I don't hate you, Diesel, not at all. Actually, I really like you. I mean, if I weren't the therapist at your school, if we somehow knew each other in a different way, I can guarantee that this little visit of yours would have gone a completely different way." Greg started rubbing Diesel's back with both hands. Diesel stepped in and again pressed his body into Greg's and whispered in his ear, "Please, Doc, can't we just pretend we're two guys who just met?"

For the second time, Greg pushed Diesel away, "No, Diesel, we can't. You really should go now."

Diesel's arms dropped to his sides, "Well, can I use your bathroom before I go?"

"Sure."

Greg fell back on the chair actually shaking a bit from nerves. He wondered what had gone wrong with the script he'd carefully planned out. Diesel was going to leave! He leaned forward, elbows on his knees, his hands holding his head as he stared straight down. He heard the flush of the toilet and began to frantically try and come up with some idea that would get Diesel to stay. He was so horny that there was no way he was going to let that slab of meat get away from him. He heard the bathroom door open.

"Doc?"

Greg looked up and froze. Diesel had taken off the sweat clothes. He was clad in a red wrestling singlet, the same bright red as his boots. Diesel walked slowly across the room toward Greg — it seemed like he was walking in slow motion. Greg felt paralyzed. All he could do was stare at Diesel, unblinking. Things gradually began to enter his brain.

He realized that the singlet's material was different...it wasn't nylon. "What is it?" he thought. It was shiny and appeared to be seamless. It appeared so thin and stretched so tight over Diesel's body that without the occasional tiny ripples appearing in the material as he walked, Greg would have assumed that Diesel's skin had just been painted red to match the boots. Greg had never seen someone wearing something that was this form fitting.

And then his eyes fell to Diesel's crotch and he saw the proof that it wasn't just painted skin. Diesel's mammoth monster cock was pointed down along his left leg, encased in whatever the material was. His enormous balls were bulging next to each other on the right side like two goose eggs resting next to each other. Diesel walked up to the seated doctor, stopping about a foot away from him, his legs touching the insides of Greg's spread legs on the chair. Greg's head was about level with Diesel's abs, but all he could stare at was that cock...that living, breathing monster...the hog.

"I really do like you, doc, a lot. And I want the chance to show you how much I like you. Can I stay...please?" asked Diesel as he brought his hands up to his waist.

Leather! That's what it was. The faint musky aroma filled Greg's nostrils. This close, he could make out a very tiny seam running up and down the center of the singlet. The hog released its magnet on Greg's eyes allowing Greg to look up at Diesel's smiling face, "Where in fuck's name did you get this outfit?"

"There's this old guy — he likes to give me massages and shit like that. He's got lots of money and buys lots of clothes for me and even has a few things custom made, like this. He likes to take pictures of me in them. It's some kind of special leather that's super thin but still really strong. There are only a few zippers in the whole thing and they're made out of some kind of special metal or plastic or something. You're supposed to not really be able to see them much, supposed to be like a second skin or something," said Diesel as he rubbed his hands up and down the red material covering his abs, "You like?"

Greg dumbly nodded his head up and down while trying to take in the whole red package of muscle.

"Go ahead, doc...go ahead," whispered Diesel as he saw Greg's hands shifting at his sides. Greg wasn't sure what he wanted to do first. He placed a hand on the upper outside thigh of each leg. The first thing he noticed was how warm the red material was, and then he noticed as he slowly started rubbing up and down in a circular motion, half the time rubbing the leather, half the time rubbing the bare skin of Diesel's leg beneath the seamless cuff of the singlet, that the leather seemed smoother and softer than Diesel's skin. He liked how it all felt, letting out a groan of appreciation. His hands moved further back to the hard mass that made up Diesel's very impressive ass. Another moan escaped Greg's lips as Diesel flexed his glutes over and over, letting Greg feel the ass muscles moving as he rubbed his hands over the leather covered mounds. Greg's eyes were shut and his head hung lazily backwards. Greg felt something touch his upper lip and opened his eyes, staring straight up at the blond god towering above him. Diesel was running a thumb around Greg's partially open mouth.

"The hog, doc. What about the hog?" asked Diesel tenderly. Greg's eyes were pulled to Diesel's cock. He could tell that it was still soft, but he couldn't get over its size. He'd already seen it more than once in the flesh, but the sheer length and girth of it, encased in the thin layer of bright red leather just inches from his face, seemed impossible to be real. And yet, he knew it was real...and it was there...inches away from him...waiting for him. Greg's hands slid slowly from the rippling ass muscles to the hips to the front of the thighs. Greg held his breath as both hands landed on the hot soft mass of tubesteak. Diesel let out a soft sigh of air.

Greg's hands rubbed lightly back and forth along the tube's length a number of times, then as one hand kept up the pace, the other moved to the side to caress Diesel's warm soft goose eggs. Though the leather was stretched smooth across all of Diesel, it was also very pliable and Greg slowly juggled Diesel's nuts in his hand. They were big enough that Greg couldn't hold both of them in one hand at the same time.

He felt a tap on his head and looked up. Diesel had unzipped the micro-zipper that went down the front of the singlet. He stopped when his hand hit the top of Greg's head. Greg saw the red leather stretched open in a "V" pattern, down to Diesel's pubic hair, revealing the bulk of Diesel's chest and slicing through his bulging abs.

"You like my chest, Doc?" asked Diesel with excitement in his eyes.

Greg stood up from the chair, stopping part way up when his mouth was level with Diesel's chest and he licked the hot skin. He licked up the valley between the masses of pec flesh. He licked again... and again. He brought a hand to each mound, grabbing the flesh as he started to lick the trench faster. Diesel guided Greg's mouth to his left nipple. Greg took the bait and started sucking on the mass, gravitating to the nipple. It hardened the instant Greg's hot breath came near it; Diesel sucked in air through clenched teeth.

Greg pressed his crotch onto Diesel's thigh and groaned as he continued to suck on the nipple. Diesel pulled Greg's face off his chest, "Don't you like it more than that, Doc? Go ahead, show that tit who's boss." Greg shot forward and grabbed the nipple between his teeth and started to chew on it.

"Oh, yeah, that's right...that's right...that's right...," Diesel kept mumbling as he threw his head back and rubbed the back of Greg's head, pulling the head a bit more into his chest.

"Would you do me a favor, Doc? I like it a little rough. Would you pound my chest a bit? It really makes me feel good."

Greg lifted his head slowly away from the pec. A stream of spit joined his mouth to it breaking after a few inches. He looked up at Diesel's smiling face, and while still looking at him, gave Diesel's left pec a punch with his right fist. Diesel's head pulsed a jump in reaction, his smile broadened a bit.

Greg punched the other pec. He then started pummeling the chest with blow after blow, hearing the thuds and thinking how he was mimicking what Danny got to do and that made him even hotter. Diesel's hands went to Greg's firm ass and pulled their crotches together. Suddenly Diesel let go of Greg's ass, grabbed his head, and firmly planted a kiss on his doctor, shoving his tongue into Greg's silky mouth. Greg's arms fell to his sides as he gave into the pleasure of the tongue exploration. Diesel broke the kiss, held Greg's head inches from his, and whispered, "The hog, doc...the hog wants some attention."

Greg let his open mouth ride over the lumps of Diesel's chest and abs travelling down to a kneeling position on his journey to the prize. The leather was open down to the base of the soft torpedo which snaked its way under the thin leather coating down Diesel's left thigh. Greg's hands came to join his mouth, but Diesel grabbed Greg's wrists, "Doc, try doin' it with just your mouth, 'kay?"

Without bothering to look up, Greg dropped his arms and loosely wrapped them around Diesel's calves and started his frantic search to free the hog. He used his nose and tongue, pushing, pulling and grunting into Diesel's crotch. Diesel looked down from above with a smirk as he played with his own nipples.

After more than a few minutes of frustrating labors, it dawned on Greg that if he could find the miniscule zipper, he'd be able to pull it down more and let him win his prize. He followed the almost invisible ridge of one side of the zipper with the skin of his nose to where the ridge joined the other edge. Not being able to distinguish any kind of tab, Greg decided to press down with his nose where the ridges met. He'll dully felt his nose sting, not realizing that the zipper, though tiny, was made of a very hard alloy, and its sharpness scraped skin off Greg's nose. He was in the heat of passion and could have cared less.

He felt the zipper opening more and more. When he was about to relieve his nose of the pain, a jolt of sexual pleasure shot through his body as he felt Diesel's cock land with a thud on his head. He pulled his head back, allowing the cock to fall off his head and swing down in front of his face — it banged the tip of Greg's nose a few times as it slowly came to rest. He used his hands for a moment to fully free Diesel's balls so they could join the party, then wrapped his arms around Diesel's calves once again.

Squatting lower so his mouth was at the tip of Diesel's dick, he looked up to the wrestler's face, and stuck his tongue out, swiping it along Diesel's piss slit. He then ran his tongue up the length of the tube, never taking his eyes from Diesel's face where he could see the pleasure spreading across Diesel's face. Greg went back down to the tip, opened his mouth wide, and attempted to suck in the head of the hog — no such luck — it was just too big.

"It's OK, Doc, most guys can't get it in on their first try. Just relax. And besides, this is about you, not me," said Diesel as he looked down at Greg, running a couple of fingers back and forth along Greg's forehead.

This only made Greg more determined to envelope the head. Doubling his efforts, Greg tried opening his mouth even wider, pressing against the flesh of the dick, while breathing through his nose. He moaned with pleasure as he felt his lips fell over the ridge of the mushroom head.

"Oh, Doc, you are the best! Not many guys can do that so quickly."

By this time, Greg's arms had moved up and were locked on Diesel's legs just above his knees. Diesel wrapped both his hands around his own stalk and started pumping it as he instructed his doctor, "Try running your tongue all around the head. It feels great when you do that."

Greg's tongue went on its journey. He could have sworn that it was like he was feeling tremors of an earthquake as he watched Diesel's own hands moving back and forth along the pipeline, getting close to his eyes and then receding — over and over. Greg's own dick was hard, throbbing and hurting. He felt that he was on the verge of shooting without even touching himself — something he'd read about but assumed was not possible. He'd also assumed a dick the size of Diesel's was not possible, so he gave into the pleasures shooting through his crotch.

Letting go of his dick, Diesel's hands moved to Greg's head and started trying to help more of his pole into the doctor's wet warm mouth. Up to this point, Greg was relatively comfortable accommodating Diesel's unit. At least, his sexual frenzy had allowed him to reach this point. But as more of the cock squeezed its way into his mouth, Greg started to panic, his jaw was hurting and he felt his air passages were going to be cut off.

He squeezed Diesel's legs, looked up, his eyes bulging, face and neck bright red, with veins in his neck standing out. Diesel looked down at the doctor with a dreamy smile on his face as he pulled harder on Greg's head. With what he felt were his last moments of consciousness, Greg began gagging and pulling his head back.

Suddenly he was free. His back slammed into the wooden chair he'd been sitting on, knocking it over. He brought his hands to his neck and leaning down, he coughed and hacked repeatedly.

"Doctor Thompson! Doctor Thompson! I am so sorry! I didn't mean to hurt you. Sometimes guys really like it when I force myself into them. Some of them really like to even pass out! I thought maybe that's what you wanted since you were able to get the whole head in on your own. Oh, Doc, I am so so sorry!"

When Greg calmed down to where his breathing was almost back to normal he looked up at Diesel who stood there with a look on his face like he was a puppy who'd just shit on the rug. Greg immediately felt sorry for the kid. Besides, he looked so good standing there with a stream of Greg's mucus hanging from the tip of Diesel's cock.

"It's OK, Diesel, the hog here seems to have a mind of its own," said Greg with a smile as he grabbed the monster with one hand, fingering the head. Diesel leaned down, put a hand in each of Greg's armpits, pulled him to a standing position and gently pressed his crotch to Greg's.

"What's say we move this into the bedroom and give your knees a rest?" said Diesel as he gently planted kisses over Greg's face.

He reached inside the front of Greg's shorts and caressed the hard dick inside.

"Hey, Doctor Thompson, let him out for some playtime," and then pushed down Greg's shorts. Greg stepped away and quickly shed the shorts and pullover shirt, "It's over there, Diesel...lead the way." The red leather singlet, from the back, made Diesel's shoulders look extremely wide and whatever his waist size was, it looked impossibly tiny compared to the space that the kid's shoulders took up.

Diesel fell down on his back on the queen sized bed, legs spread, arms reaching up toward Greg. Greg climbed on top of his client, sliding his hands inside the open leather singlet to the warm flesh of Diesel's back as the two fought each other with their tongues.

"I've got an idea, Doc. Let me tie you to the bed. I've learned a lot about what turns guys on and I really really want to make you feel good. All you'd have to do is say the word and the ties would come off, but once you see what I can do for you, I bet you'll be asking for stuff other than that."

"Everything is going as planned," thought Greg with a smile. He knew that he'd only heard the tip of the iceberg from Diesel while he was hypnotized about the stuff he did with other men — the stuff other men paid him to do. The thought of talking Diesel through some of these things, and doing some of them, really excited Greg.

"Sure, Diesel, I think that's a great idea."

From out of nowhere, Diesel produced four strips of the same red leather as his singlet and tied each wrist to the outside post of the bed's metal headboard, and each ankle to the other end of the bed. The whole time he talked to Greg about things he would do to him and he kept kissing and rubbing different parts of Greg's body. Greg was in heaven. His rock hard seven inches rested on his respectable six pack.

"God! You look good enough to eat, Doctor Thompson!" said Diesel, standing at the foot of the bed staring at his naked spread-eagled therapist. As he locked eyes with Greg, he slowly climbed onto the bed and started crawling up Greg's body. When he was flat on top of him, he held his face a few inches about Greg's, whispered, "Now, where were we?" and then dove in for a passionate kiss. Greg groaned his approval. He also realized that one thing he now couldn't do was run his hands all over Diesel's body. But as Diesel said, this was going to be about pleasuring Greg, and Greg would make sure that happened.

"Wait a minute. That's not where we were," said Diesel, breaking the kiss and lifting his face from Greg's, "I had something else in your mouth. Now what was it? It wasn't my tongue...I remember! It was the hog!" Greg chuckled at Diesel's attempt at humor.

"Yes, that fuckstick should be registered with the local authorities as an assault weapon," Greg said with a big smile. Diesel had sat up on Greg's body, his leather covered asscrack making a very pleasant warmer for Greg's hard-on. Diesel scooted forward, sliding off Greg's cock, his own flaccid but intimidating member lumbered forward across Greg's abs and chest toward his head. The tip hit Greg's chin, who was patiently lying flat on the bed, eager for more fun to happen.

"Oops. The Mars Rover has hit an obstacle. Let's see if backing up and coming forward again will help," said Diesel as be scooted back a bit then shoved forward further than before, his cock flopping upward, the head landing on Greg's lips. Greg's smile changed to an open mouth as his tongue lifted up to coat as much of the mushroom head he could reach.

"Houston! Houston! We have proof that Mars has water even now!" said Diesel with a smile as he pushed his dickhead into Greg's mouth. Greg's laugh was cut short with the head popping into his mouth.

"Do the tongue thing again, Doc," said Diesel in a heavy whisper as he massaged the sides of Greg's head. Greg was happy to oblige and was rewarded by a long loan moan from Diesel, who then forced a bit more of the hog in. Greg wasn't too worried and responded by continuing his tongue rotations. He could feel his own pulsing dick leaking precum.

But when Diesel pushed forward again, Greg took notice and tried to spit the monster out. Diesel's eyes were shut and he moaned again as he felt Greg's tongue moving more rapidly around the hog, pushing a jabbing at it. Greg started to choke and couldn't seem to get Diesel's attention, so he brought his teeth slightly together, clamping onto the intruder.

Diesel let out a yelp and pulled his dick of out Greg's mouth.

"Sorry I did that, Diesel," said Greg through heaving breaths, "but I was starting to choke and couldn't get your attention."

Greg felt the hard sting of a slap on the side of his face and before he could figure it out, he felt another on the other side of his face. Two hands then clamped one on either side of his head, above his ears.

"Nobody ever uses teeth on the hog!" shouted Diesel is a voice so loud, Greg momentarily forgot the sting of the slaps. Diesel was staring at Greg, his head literally quivering in anger.

"Diesel...calm down. I was scared...I couldn't breathe...and I couldn't get your attention. I think maybe it would be better if you untied me...now," said Greg.

"Untie you...now? Is that an order, Doctor Thompson?" asked Diesel with a genuine snarl in his voice.

"Actually, Diesel, yes...it is an order. Untie me," said Greg, looking at Diesel.

"Oh, that's right. This is the point where I'm supposed to listen to what you tell me to do. What was it? 'You'll do everything I tell you to do', was that it, Doctor...was that what you said to me a few hours ago?" asked Diesel, his lips curled menacingly.

Greg stared, speechless.

"Cat got your tongue, Doc? Hope not...cause I'm gonna be having you use it plenty tonight."

"Diesel...I don't understand...what are you talking about?" asked Greg, genuinely scared. He had to find a way out of this.

"I'm talkin' about all that shit you said and did while you thought I was hypnotized. Yeah, 'thought', that's the word I used. You're nothin' but a pathetic piece of shit. So hot for me, you didn't care that you were supposed to be doin' a job.

Ya know...I'm a college kid who needs help," said Diesel sarcastically. "Well, you had your fun with me, now I'm gonna have my fun with you. Don't worry, no permanent damage. And every once in a while, you're actually gonna feel good. But most of the time, you're gonna be nothin' but my cum container. Got that? I said, got that?" asked Diesel as he accompanied the second 'got that' with another slap to Greg's face.

"No, Diesel, I don't. You'd better let me up now or you may do something that will have severe consequences to your permanent record."

Diesel laughed.

"Permanent record? You think I give a flying fuck about my permanent record? It's your permanent record we're lookin' at here, asshole. I got just about all our sessions on tape. That gym bag holds lots of stuff. I could let you decide if I should give them to the college president or directly to one or two College Station papers so they could hear every word and grunt. Huh? What do you think that would do to your permanent record? Now just shut the fuck up. I'm really tired of playing all the games I did to get you to this point. You're gonna do what I say when I say.

You're my cumrag, you're my pussyboy, you're my toilet, you're my toy. Now, I'll ask again, got that?" This whole time, Diesel was on his knees, slowly dragging the tip of his dick in a circle underneath Greg's chin, along his cheek, across an eye, over the nose, and down again.

Diesel took his dick in his hand and slapped the side of Greg's head with it, "I didn't quite hear that, Doc. What did you say?"

"Yes, I got it. But please, Diesel...." Greg was cut off with the hardest slap yet to his face.

"You didn't understand the 'shut the fuck up' part?"

Greg slowly nodded his head, his opened eyes wide with fear. Diesel smiled in return, noting the red finger marks his last slap made on Greg's cheek.

"OK, now I want you to get a good look at the hog. He goes where he wants to go and does what he wants to do. I show him a lot of respect and I expect you to do the same. Got it?" Diesel held his cock in his hand waving it above Greg's face. Greg nodded.

"Now before we begin, kiss it. Kiss it right here," Diesel pointed to a spot on his dick that was slightly discolored...a purple/yellow color... the probable remnants of a bruise. Greg pursed his lips and Diesel pressed the flesh against Greg's mouth.

"Oh...and the bruise? I bet you're wondering about that. That from Danny's chewin'? I wonder. Now did I make up the whole story about me and Danny or did it happen? You know what, Doc, I really can't seem to remember. It's kinda foggy for me. But how else could that bruise have gotten there?" Diesel began rubbing the length of his dick around Greg's face.

"Maybe me and Mr. Peters do stuff that would cause a bruise. Remember...he pays me a lot to do stuff. Or maybe it was somebody else chewin' on my stalk. Maybe some hot to trot cop, marine, jock, or maybe it was some other kind of doctor. Maybe I even bruised it slamming it around while dancin' naked for a bunch a fags in a bar. Maybe you can bruise it another way. Maybe you can bruise it usin' it to teach a lesson. What do you think, Doc?" asked Diesel as he started slapping Greg's face with his cock.

The slaps came quicker and harder. Greg shut his eyes. It was starting to hurt. It finally stopped and Greg opened his eyes to see a panting Diesel staring down at him.

"You know what, Doc. I can tell ya, it would hurt you more if it was hard. You're lucky. Now, back to taking care of the hog." Diesel squatted back down and put the tip of his dick at Greg's lips.

"Oh, I almost forgot. The hog feels any teeth...at any point...and there will be some permanent damage. Open up, doc. The probe needs to do further research on the soil."

Greg surrendered and parted his lips. Diesel shoved forward jamming his cockhead into Greg's mouth. He reached down and caressed the side of Greg's face, "That a boy." He shoved more in...and more...and more.

Greg's face turned red and he choked. Diesel pulled back, not to solve the choking, but because he wanted to start the old in and out motion that would soon have his rocket, rock hard. He jammed his dick in again...out...in...out...in. No matter how hard he pushed, less than a third of his dick would enter the wet cavern. Tears streamed out of Greg's eyes uncontrollably as he continued to choke.

"I got the wrong angle, buddy, gotta change so the hog can finish his mission," said Diesel as he pulled his dick out of Greg's mouth and stayed above Greg for a moment, his half hard dick swaying left and right as Greg coughed up phlegm, splattering much of it on the hog. Diesel quickly flipped himself and scooted back so he could enter Greg's mouth from above. He knew from experience that aiming his dick down the same angle as his worshipper's throat could sometimes allow more penetration.

"Now when I go in, I want you to be lookin' at my fine ass. It's gonna stay covered in leather. You're not worthy enough to see it in the flesh, but you can dream all you want while you watch it flex as I pump in and out of your mouth. Got it, pussyboy?"

"Yes," whispered Greg.

Diesel reached between his legs, his knees pinning the already tied down arms of Greg to the bed, and guided his cock into Greg's mouth that opened on cue.

"Sweet Jesus!" exclaimed Diesel when on his first thrust, got half his dick into Greg's throat. He felt the muscles closed at the back of Greg's throat and pushed against them.

"Open up, fuckbreath, open up." Diesel pulled out and shoved in again. He started pile driving into Greg's face. Greg couldn't breathe and his body shook as he choked. Diesel pulled out and looked down between his legs. The sight got him really hot. His fat dick hung above Greg's face, dripping Greg's juices from the tip of his prick back onto Greg's neck, while Greg coughed and sprayed phlegm outward, again, some splattering onto the dangling battering ram. All Diesel saw was more lubrication that would make his journey to paradise smoother. He jammed the hog back in the hot wet cave. This time well over half got inside.

Though thinking he could die at any moment, Greg couldn't help remembering Diesel's words about his ass. Most of the time, Greg focused on trying to breathe, but he also took the time to look at Diesel's asscheeks as the musclegod slammed into his mouth over and over. And with all the pain, part of Greg's brain registered the draw of seeing those leather covered cheeks pucker in and out as the dick in front of them plowed in and out of his mouth.

Three more times during his jackrabbit fucking of Greg's mouth, Diesel pulled out and watched the combined spit and precum drip back onto Greg, while Greg struggled to get his breathing back. After about 20 minutes, Diesel was ready to drop a load. He didn't know if Greg was conscious or not — he didn't really care. He just wanted to spray his sperm into Greg's stomach — and he did — braying like a bull with each pump of fluid.

As soon as he recovered, Diesel flipped around again, this time sitting on Greg's thighs facing him. Greg's head was rocking sideways, as his coughing fit gradually subsided. A mixture of his own spit and Diesel's cum ran down his face from each corner of his mouth.

"That was fun, wasn't it, Doc?" asked Diesel as he started playing with Greg's flaccid cock, "let's see what other fun we can have."

Diesel grabbed both pillows that had fallen onto the floor during his athletic face fuck and shoved them roughly underneath the strapped down therapist at the base of his spine, stretching his tied down arms and legs. This also caused his pelvis, cock and balls to bulge upward on display. Diesel kept up the fondling of Greg's dick.

Greg was certainly not comfortable with the leather straps pulling at both wrists and ankles. The pillows forcing his pelvis forward were not painful, just awkward feeling.

Diesel positioned himself at the end of the bed, squatted between Greg's spread legs. He was half hard and his dick swayed menacingly. He put a paw on either of Greg's thighs, said, "Look at me, you cumrag," squatted a bit more and forced his dickhead into Greg's unlubricated asshole. Greg howled in pain and he pulled away as hard as he could — which wasn't far.

"What's the matter, Doc? Did I take advantage of our therapist/ client relationship just now? Wondering what's coming next? Will I go balls to the wall?" Diesel asked with a smile. His hands travelled up and down Greg's thighs. In spite of the fear racing through his body, Greg was hard.

"No, Doc, I'm not gonna do that...just yet. I'm not the kind of asshole who takes advantages inappropriately," said Diesel as he pulled his dickhead out of Greg's ass. Greg was surprised that the first thing his brain focused on was the feeling of emptiness in his ass. Diesel knelt so that his lower legs were spread across each of Greg's thighs and reached for Greg's hard cock.

"It's time you got to feel some good. That OK with you, Doc?"

"Yes...Diesel," Greg replied tentatively. Diesel moved forward a bit and made sure his dick and balls pressed into the pillows propping up Greg, and his pelvis pressed just underneath Greg's balls. With one hand he pumped Greg's dick up and down, while the other one roamed over his own torso.

"C'mon, Greg, it won't take you long. Shoot your load...on me...on this," said Diesel as his fingertips ran up and down his abs. "Shoot a load of frosting all over this Diesel cake in front of you. Gimme a thick creamy layer of frosting."

Greg couldn't take his eyes off of Diesel's hand that was roaming around his body. Watching Diesel caress his own muscles was getting Greg to his climax faster than he'd ever travelled to one. He suddenly stiffened and splattered his frosting over the front of Diesel.

"Oh, yeah, that must have felt real good, Doc. Your face was something to see while you were squirtin' your load. And look... you did just like I told you. Look at your cum all over my abs. Mmmmmmm, it feels so warm on my skin."

Diesel let go of Greg's dick and moved both his hands gently around his own skin, spreading the cum a bit. Then he started scooping it up off his skin as best he could and moved back slightly.

"Nothing like a steamy load of cum as lubrication," said Diesel as he began coating his dick with Greg's cum. "Look, that's your spunk all over the hog," said Diesel as he held his staff up with one hand for Greg to see, and moved his other cum covered hand to Greg's asscrack, giving it a good coating.

"Diesel, wait, I thought you said you weren't one to take advantage. You're not going to fuck me, are you?" asked Greg nervously.

"I'm not taking advantage. You got off, didn't you? Fair is fair. And remember, I could have fucked you dry. The hog wouldn't have cared much. But I wanted to show you a little mercy." Greg's eyes squeezed shut as Diesel once again forced the head of his dick in.

"OK, Doc. Your turn. Help me in. I can shove it in on my own, but I don't think you'd like that. You help me, and we can go slow and let things move out of the hog's way. Relax. Let us in, Doc, we'll take you for a ride you won't forget."

Greg relaxed his ass muscles and saw stars as his ass was slowly invaded by the giant cylinder. He'd never felt this full of a feeling in his life. Diesel started moving in and out of the steamy hot tunnel of flesh. He took Greg's cock in one hand and started jacking it all over again, using his other hand to rub his own chest.

"Doc! Look at me. I'm fucking you good. How does it feel? Look at this body that's connected to the dick that's taking you on a balloon ride to where there's no oxygen," said Diesel as he pumped at his therapist's ass.

"C'mon, Doc, let's cum again. I know you can do it. Focus on my body. Look at this muscleboy who's so hot for you, he'd like to fuck you for days without stopping."

Greg hardened with Diesel's encouragement. He really was amazed at the muscles on this kid. If only he could touch them...lick them... he'd shoot off immediately. By now, Diesel's body was not just covered with sweat, it was rolling off him like a waterfall. Greg kept staring at Diesel, impressed that he could fuck so long and keep up a constant stream of gutter talk.

"Doc, I need you to drop another load. You gotta fire off another one," said Diesel as he yanked harder and harder on Greg's dick. Diesel just wanted to milk Greg — wanted to teach him a lesson. He was counting on the fact that Greg's lust for Diesel would be stronger than anything else. Diesel started rotating his hips slightly as he moved in and out. It had the double effect on Greg of the hog venturing into some unexplored territory and the sight of Diesel's sensual movements put Greg over the edge. It wasn't as powerful a shoot as his first load of course and the majority of it ended up spread around Diesel's fist that coaxed the load out.

"Good job, buddy!" said Diesel as he let go of Greg's cock, lifted his hand in the air and flicked the sperm juices onto Greg's body. "And the hog really likes it when he's inside some guy's shitchute and the guy cums. You know the way your ass muscles squeeze when you cum? Yeah, the hog really likes getting those love squeezes," said Diesel as he continued fucking Greg. By this time, Diesel had no trouble getting his entire dick inside Greg's ass. He was relishing the feeling because it wasn't often a guy could take all of him.

"OK, Doc, we're gonna go for another one," said Diesel as he grabbed Greg's softening cock is one of his paws.

"No, Diesel, please...I can't," whispered a very tired, scared and sweaty Greg.

"No can do, Senor Thompson, three is the magic number. We have to hit it. You can do it, little man. You can squeeze out another load. Look, you're already getting hard again," Diesel said with a big smile.

Greg knew that it was just biology, physics and his own lust at work, it wasn't really a choice. This amazingly hot college kid talking dirty, fucking him with a quarterstaff, playing with his dick, and putting himself on display was something Greg's sexual urges couldn't ignore.

"And besides, the hog wants those love squeezes again. It's really hard to say no to the hog when he's on a mission. Know what I mean, Doc?"

By this time, Greg was hard again...and it hurt. But Greg couldn't help staring at the mass of muscles, drenched in sweat, in front of him, and that meant he couldn't help from getting and staying hard.

"Tell ya what. We're a partnership and I should contribute something," said Diesel as he let go of Greg's dick, reached up with both hands, pulled the singlet's leather shoulder straps off, and pulled the singlet way down on either side so that the only part of his body left covered with it were his legs. He took hold of Greg's dick again and reached around back of himself with his other hand.

"Can you see that long mirror on the back of you bedroom door? Go ahead, stretch a bit to the side and see if you can."

Greg leaned as far to his right as the leather straps and pillows jammed under his back would allow and was able to see the full length mirror on the partially open bedroom door; it was not a comfortable position. His eyes widened.

"Yeah...you can see it, can't you? That's my ass — in the flesh. Nice hard big college wrestler ass...isn't it? Don't you wish that was your hand rubbing it?" Diesel was really enjoying teasing Greg. He kept up a steady rhythm of masturbating Greg's tool with his other hand.

"Watch this," said Diesel as he started rubbing his free hand up and down his asscrack. The skin was quite wet, sweat having collected there while encased under the red leather.

"Oh, does that feel good...." Diesel could feel Greg's dick pulsing as he rubbed its length. It was working. Time for the next level.

"Ohhhhh, God!" came out of Greg's mouth as he watched Diesel shove his index finger up his own ass. He glanced at Diesel's face and saw his eyes shut tightly and then stretched back to the mirror so he wouldn't miss anything. The finger was going in and out. Greg's breathing became rapid. Diesel pulled his finger out of his ass, brought it up to his nose, took a long smell, and leaned forward stretching his hand toward Greg's face. Greg was panting. Diesel kept his eyes on Greg's face, smiling, continuing the dick jacking.

"Cum!" ordered Diesel as he shoved the finger into Greg's mouth. With a gurgled scream, neck veins bulging, Greg pumped out his third load in less than an hour. It wasn't much, and he whimpered feeling the few last dry pumps of his orgasm.

"Wow! That must have felt awesome, huh, Doc?" said Diesel as he climbed off the bed, pulled the singlet completely off and threw it on a chair. He walked up to the side of the bed standing near one of Greg's outstretched arms. He lifted his resting cock and flopped it onto Greg's lower arm and began sliding it back and forth.

"I lied Doc. The magic number is four. You're not gonna disappoint me and the hog now, are you?" he asked with a smile as he continued to slide his dick, now up and down the entire length of Greg's arm, stopping short of his hand and poking his armpit with his cocktip each time he got to that end.

"Diesel...I can't...I really can't...please...don't make me...."

"It's just a case of mind over matter. Here, I'll help you even more this time," said Diesel as he really surprised Greg by climbing on top of him. Greg was revived a bit as he felt the wrestler's body make contact with his. Among all the sweat and cum on them, there was no need to think about any kind of lubrication needed between them. Diesel pressed his body on top of Greg's, legs on legs, cock on cock, and Diesel's massive arms stretched along Greg's. Diesel hands grasped Greg's. He started pressing his pelvis into Greg's, whispering all sorts of filthy words into Greg's ear, getting Greg hard as he rotated his pelvis against Greg's.

Greg figured he was about to die from sexual exhaustion and gave into it. He was becoming delusional with the stimulation he was feeling all over. What he really wanted to do was feel Diesel's body with his hands. He wanted to rub his hands all over it. He wanted to feel all those muscles working and shifting.

Diesel just wanted to see if he could get a fourth load out of this guy. He was determined to get it. Without realizing how much he was in sync with Greg, he thought that maybe if he untied Greg's arms, that would put him over the edge. He reached up and quickly yanked at the leather straps at Greg's wrists. (Little did Greg know,

Diesel had used a knot that he could have easily gotten out of by pulling on either end of the knot.)

"Go for it, faggot!" whispered Diesel into Greg's ear when he untied him. Greg's brain registered that his arms were suddenly free. Nearly delirious with exhaustion and sexual frenzy, Greg was running on instinct. That instinct told him that he was near a climax. He was hurting, but he was ready to fire. His hands shot forward, each grabbing one of Diesel's asscheeks, feeling them dimple with each press Diesel gave into Greg's crotch.

"Juice me up, Doc, squeeze my ass and shoot your fuckin' load!"

"Aaaaaaggggggggghhhhhhhh!" came the ragged reply from Greg as his muscles flexed painfully, a drop or two of cum were forced out of his dick. His hands slid off Diesel's hard glutes, and he passed out.

Diesel jumped off the bed, walked over to Greg's computer and typed on the screen:

Greg: Thanks. You're a hell of a fuck. Hope there are no hard feelings. I'll be back tomorrow night, wearing something I think you'll like. I'll bring something for you to wear too. What do you like? Denim? Leather? Latex? Nylon? Cotton? Metal? You look kind of like a latex guy. We'll see. Maybe I'll let you fuck me — think about it. D.

Diesel picked up his red leather singlet and walked out of the bedroom.

"Night's still young — maybe I'll go to the bar and dance a bit. This leather outfit should get me some nice tips...oh yeah," Diesel thought as he put on his sweat clothes and walked out the door.

ABOUT THE AUTHOR

Allen Giffen

Allen Giffen is new to the world of erotic writing. He hopes you enjoy his efforts.